Violet's Foreign Intrigue

Violet's Foreign Intrigue

BOOK EIGHT
of the
A Life of Faith:
Violet Travilla
Series

Based on the characters by
Martha Finley

MCP
Mission City Press

Franklin, Tennessee

Book Eight of the *A Life of Faith: Violet Travilla* Series

Violet's Foreign Intrigue
Copyright © 2006, Mission City Press, Inc. All Rights Reserved.

Published by Mission City Press, Inc.

This book is based on the *Elsie Dinsmore* series written by Martha Finley and first published in 1868 by Dodd, Mead & Company.

Cover & Interior Design: Richmond & Williams
Cover Photography: Michelle Grisco Photography
Typesetting: BookSetters

For more information, write to Mission City Press at 202 Second Avenue South, Franklin, Tennessee 37064, or visit our Web Site at: **www.alifeoffaith.com.**

For a FREE catalog call 1-800-840-2641.

Library of Congress Catalog Card Number: 2005924798
Finley, Martha
          Violet's Foreign Intrigue
          Book Eight of the *A Life of Faith: Violet Travilla* Series
          Hardcover: ISBN-10: 1-928749-24-0
                                  ISBN-13: 978-1-928749-24-0
          Softcover: ISBN-10: 1-934306-08-8
                                  ISBN:-13: 978-1-934306-08-6

Printed in the United States of America
4 5 6 7 8 9 10 — 11 10 09 08 07

— FOREWORD —

*P*romises that were made in previous volumes of Vi Travilla's story will be kept in this, the eighth novel in the *A Life of Faith: Violet Travilla* series. A family is formed, three children will get their wish, and an astonishing adventure will take them all to a tropical isle far to the south of their comfortable home in India Bay. Though many difficulties for Vi and her loved ones have been resolved, there are new dilemmas to confront and new characters whose motives may — or may not — be worthy of Vi's trust. Vi's most unexpected challenge will be to unravel a web of secrets and protect those closest to her from grave harm.

Violet's Foreign Intrigue, like all the books in the Violet series, is based on characters created in the second half of the nineteenth century by Miss Martha Finley. Miss Finley achieved wide acclaim for her many novels focusing on young people and their struggles to live their Christian faith in a time of momentous change. Through literature, Miss Finley encouraged and inspired millions of young Christians and their parents to hold fast to their biblical principles, no matter what trials and temptations faced them. Mission City Press is very proud to continue Miss Finley's mission in this series of new stories built on the timeless foundations of faith, love, and hope.

∽ THE ISLANDS AND THE PIRATES OF THE CARIBBEAN ∽

The island of Christiana, where *Violet's Foreign Intrigue* takes place, is entirely imaginary. It is a fictional composite of features of many of the islands of the Caribbean.

The Caribbean Sea is a part of the Atlantic Ocean; it is a basin of more than a million square miles bordered by parts of Central and South America and a crescent-shaped string of islands. This archipelago of islands stretches for more than two thousand miles from near Florida to the northern coast of Venezuela in South America.

Christopher Columbus, who was Italian by birth, sailed west from Spain with three ships and first set foot in the "New World" on October 12, 1492. He was not the first European to reach the Americas, but his voyage set off a great wave of exploration, conquest, and immigration that literally changed world history. Columbus first landed on an island in the Bahamas called *Guanahini* by the native people but renamed San Salvador by the Spaniards. From there, he sailed on to Cuba, the largest of the Caribbean islands, and Hispaniola (now Haiti and the Dominican Republic). He claimed these islands and all the territories he found on his three subsequent voyages for the King and Queen of Spain, who financed his explorations. Because Columbus believed that he had reached Asia, he called the original inhabitants "Indians" and the islands "Indies." These names, although inaccurate, stuck, and to this day, the Caribbean islands are referred to as the West Indies.

When Columbus returned to Spain with reports of natives decked out in gold jewelry, he set the stage for a period of conquest for wealth. But on his second voyage to the Indies, in 1493, he also brought the sources for a new agricultural economy. His ships carried livestock; grain, vegetable, and fruit seeds; citrus trees; and vines. Most important, he introduced sugar cane to the islands. Some plants imported from Europe, like wheat, did not do well in the island soil, but sugar cane thrived. After it became clear that the islands did not, after all, have much gold to mine, sugar eventually became the primary source of wealth.

Unfortunately, the profits from sugar and other resources of the islands and of Central and South America had few benefits to the native people, whose populations were devastated in battles with the Spanish invaders, by malnourishment and diseases brought to the islands from Europe, and through enslavement under the harshest conditions. No one knows how many natives there were when Columbus first landed, but estimates for the population of the island of Hispaniola are put at 200,000 to 300,000 in 1492. It has been estimated that just twenty years later, their numbers had been reduced to 20,000.[1]

Almost from the start, the Spanish had problems finding people to work their new island possessions. The near annihilation of the original people and the slow rate of Spanish migration led eventually to the importation of slaves.

The first slaves were sent to the Caribbean in 1501 from Spain itself — African captives who had been purchased from the Portuguese and converted to Christianity, and white indentured servants. Later in the 1500s, slaves were brought directly from Africa, legally and also by smugglers. The growth of the slave trade between Africa and the Caribbean was directly related to the cultivation of sugar. European settlers never immigrated to the islands in great numbers, so by the end of the sixteenth century, people of African heritage outnumbered white Europeans in many places.

When the Spanish discovered gold and silver in Mexico and then great reserves of silver in Peru, the West Indies became important primarily as ports-of-call, trading centers, and also as sources for beef and other agricultural supplies for the Spanish conquerors and their captive laborers in Central and South America. Every year, a large Spanish fleet (*flota*)—convoys of warships called *galleons* that escorted cargo ships loaded with silver, gold, precious jewels, and agricultural products including sugar, tobacco, and indigo—gathered at the ports of Havana, Cuba, and San Juan, Puerto Rico, to sail eastward for Spain. Spain's control of the sea lanes was not absolute, however. The great wealth carried by the Spanish ships attracted individuals who wanted to enrich themselves and nations eager to break up Spain's new empire. Open warfare was one option for the major European powers, who were in a nearly constant state of war with one another. But piracy often proved to be more effective.

Privateers and Buccaneers: Piracy can be generally defined as robbery and other illegal, often violent acts committed for private gain against ships at sea. Piracy has an ancient history and has been practiced in all parts of the world. Piracy in the Caribbean seems to have a special place in the Western imagination, in large part because of the many books and movies that, beginning in the seventeenth century and continuing today, romanticize the bold exploits of the sea raiders of the 1500s, 1600s, and 1700s.

There is a difference between pirates and privateers. *Pirates* were financed by private interests and acted on their own for personal gain, though they oftentimes enjoyed the unofficial support of their government. If pirates were captured, the government could not help them. But when they sailed on official commissions from their governments, they were *privateers*; their missions were considered legal and a portion of their spoils went to the government.

Countries with weak or small navies or whose ships were engaged on other missions often employed private ships and captains as privateers. In the 1520s, France and Spain were at war, and the French government engaged Huguenot pirates to attack Spanish treasure ships in the Caribbean and the Atlantic Ocean.

In the 1630s, a group of Frenchmen added a new word to the pirate vocabulary: *buccaneer*. They were originally settlers on Hispaniola, tough woodsmen and hunters. Their name comes from the native Arawak word *buccan* or *boucan*, an open grill used for smoking and drying meat. The Spanish drove the original buccaneers from their homes but not from the island. Inspired by the exploits of famous pirates and privateers, the buccaneers, many of them former soldiers, took their fight to the sea. They raided Spanish ships and settlements with great stealth and cunning in their small, fast, sleek ships: sloops, schooners, and brigantines. The buccaneers were known to torture anyone who resisted them, so Spanish captains often surrendered without a fight when they spotted the pirates' red or black flag—the Jolly Roger.

Buccaneer was soon applied to any sea pirate in the Caribbean, whatever his nationality. Though many buccaneers were commissioned as privateers by the warring governments of Europe, the pirates were independent in nature and never easy to control. They lived hard and dangerous lives and generally squandered their stolen spoils (booty), yet they also practiced a rough kind of democracy. Under the buccaneer code, crews elected their leaders, strictly regulated conduct at sea and on land, and developed rules for the fair division of treasure. In some cases, money was provided for the care of injured comrades. There were severe penalties for violating the codes.

By the end of the 1600s, Spanish power in the Caribbean was waning. The last great buccaneer attack was against the rich coastal city of Cartagena, Venezuela, in 1689. It seemed that the European nations were beginning to tire of their incessant warfare. Agreements, such as the Treaty of Madrid (1670) between the Spanish and English, recognized the West Indian colonies of other nations and prohibited piracy. Governments that had once supported the buccaneers now sought to eliminate them. But there was to be one last period—the four decades between 1690 and 1730—when pirates seemed to rule the seas.

This so-called "Golden Age" of piracy produced some of the best known and most fearsome pirates, men like "Blackbeard" (Edward Teach), who terrorized the southern coast of the American colonies; Bartholomew ("Black Bart") Roberts, who carried out murderous raids in the West Indies; Stede Bonnet (the "gentleman pirate"), who was tried and hanged in Charleston, South Carolina, in 1718; and even two female pirates—Anne Bonny and Mary Reade, who sailed with "Calico Jack" Rackham.

Many of the "Golden Age" pirates were former buccaneers, but few followed the buccaneer codes. Their targets were no longer the gold and silver of the Spanish. Instead, they attacked regular commercial shipping, mainly from the American colonies, the Caribbean islands, and the west coast of Africa. Far from having government sanction, they were hunted to the death by the legal authorities. Motivated by greed and often great cruelty, buccaneers were driven from the seas in a relatively short time. Piracy was not eliminated entirely (and still happens today in some parts of the world); privateering continued into the 1800s, and there was a brief flare-up of pirate activity after the War of 1812, between the United States and Britain. But the development of strong national navies, coast guards, and merchant marines in the eighteenth, nineteenth, and twentieth centuries and the enforcement of international treaties and laws have effectively brought down the Jolly Roger.

Now the pirates of the Caribbean are the stuff of legend—romanticized figures who have little in common with rough-and-tumble seamen who, for almost two and a half centuries, took lives and lost their own lives in the quest for wealth and glory. The attraction of piracy in our times is probably due to the myths of great adventure and valiant heroes, but history paints a much darker tale.

[1] Source: Eric Williams, *From Columbus to Castro: The History of the Caribbean.*

xi

TRAVILLA/DINSMORE FAMILY TREE

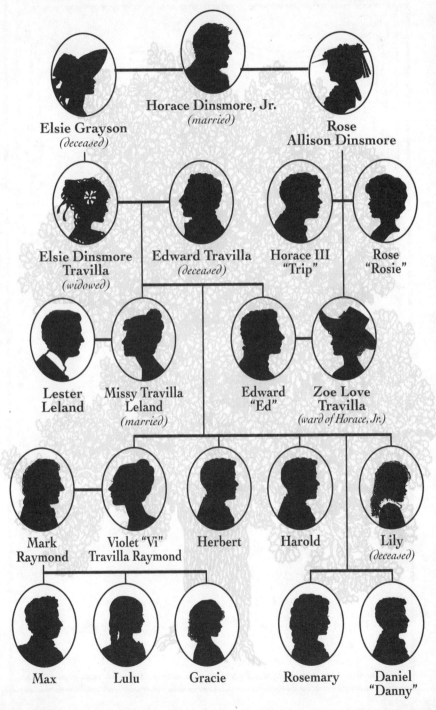

Elsie Grayson
(deceased)

Horace Dinsmore, Jr.
(married)

Rose
Allison Dinsmore

Elsie Dinsmore
Travilla
(widowed)

Edward Travilla
(deceased)

Horace III
"Trip"

Rose
"Rosie"

Lester
Leland

Missy Travilla
Leland
(married)

Edward
"Ed"

Zoe Love
Travilla
(ward of Horace, Jr.)

Mark
Raymond

Violet "Vi"
Travilla Raymond

Herbert

Harold

Lily
(deceased)

Max

Lulu

Gracie

Rosemary

Daniel
"Danny"

SETTING

*T*he story begins in February, 1886 in the southern seaport city of India Bay and proceeds to the Caribbean island of Christiana.

CHARACTERS

∞ INDIA BAY ∞

Violet Travilla Raymond (Vi) — founder of Samaritan House mission in India Bay.

Mark Raymond — husband of Vi and professor of classical languages, archaeologist, and father of
> **Max** — age 14
> **Lulu** — age 12
> **Gracie** — age 8

Mrs. Maurene O'Flaherty — Vi's dear friend and co-founder of Samaritan House.

Elsie Dinsmore Travilla — a wealthy widow and Vi's mother.

Ed Travilla — Vi's older brother, and his wife, **Zoe**.

Miss Bessie Moran — the Raymonds' housekeeper; **Kaki Kennon**, the family's young maid; and **Elwood Hogg**, the family's gardener and driver.

Polly Appleton — a friend at Samaritan House.

∞ CHRISTIANA ISLAND ∞

Dr. Hockingham — an archaeologist and professor of geology.

Malachi Bottoms — an artist.

Peter Andersen and **Elijah Berman** — assistants to Dr. Hockingham.

Thomas Barr, **Abraham Mercer**, **Liberty O'Dwyer**, and **Lorenzo Hastings** — members of the expedition team.

Sir George Dibbley — the British governor of the Christiana Islands, and his wife, **Lady Jane**.

Robert Wigham — personal secretary to the governor.

Beatrice Rowan — a maid at the governor's residence, and **Rafe**, the butler.

Reverend Smythe — vicar of the Georgetown parish, and his widowed sister, **Mrs. Smiley**.

Henry Featherstone — a cab driver.

Dr. Cowden — a physician, and **Mrs. Rita Darling**, his housekeeper and nurse.

Derrick — a villager and jungle tracker.

Colonel McTyiere — a British Army officer.

CHAPTER

1

Getting Ready for a Voyage

After saying good-by to each other, we went aboard the ship, and they returned home.

ACTS 21:6

"*W*here in the world did I put those canteens?" Vi demanded of herself as she began to unpack a large trunk she had packed just an hour earlier.

"I think you put them in that big bag of Papa's," said Lulu, who entered the dining room in time to hear Vi's question. The room, usually so neat, was littered with trunks and canvas bags and travel cases. Stacks of folded clothing covered the large dinner table, and every chair in the room was filled with items ranging from dolls and books to an odd assortment of shovels and other digging tools.

"Oh, you're right!" Vi declared with a wide smile. A strand of dark hair had tumbled down over her forehead, and she blew it back. "Thank you, darling," she said. "There's so much to pack that I can't remember what I've put where. I've packed luggage many times in my life, Lulu, but this is the first time I have had to worry about water canteens and camp stools and such. I'm so afraid I will forget something important."

Lulu looked at the clutter and asked, "What can I do to help, Mamma? There's a lot of stuff, isn't there? Will we really need all these things?"

"I expect we shall, since we will be away for four months," Vi said as she transferred a pile of freshly ironed cotton undergarments from the table to an open suitcase that she'd set on the long sideboard. "This is your bag, Lulu, so why don't you finish packing it. Then we can fill your little sister's case."

Lulu set about sorting her own clothing from among all the stacks on the table and carefully putting her things into the suitcase. Vi turned her attention to separating other items and putting them in other cases and trunks.

"We do seem to be taking a great deal," Vi laughed. "But I don't know how much shopping we'll be able to do on the island, and I don't want us running out of necessities."

"It's kinda funny to be taking all our summer clothes when it's winter," Lulu observed. "Papa explained how it's like summer all the time on Christiana Island, because it's tropical and so much closer to the Equator. But it seems strange to me—a place that doesn't have real seasons. Sometimes I have to pinch myself, Mamma, just so I'll know that we're really going there."

Lulu did pinch herself, lightly on the arm. "Ouch!" she giggled. "Yep, it's real. I'm not dreaming. We're packing for an adventure, just as Papa promised us."

The cause of Lulu's excited anticipation was the Raymonds' impending departure from their cozy home in India Bay. In another two days, the family would board a steamship that would take them on a southward journey through the Atlantic Ocean to the Christianas, a cluster of isles in the Caribbean Sea. There Lulu's father, Professor Mark Raymond, would lead a group of scholars on an archae-ological expedition in search of evidence of an ancient culture.

"Do you think Papa will find what he's looking for?" Lulu asked as she laid several folded blouses in her suitcase.

"I hope he will," Vi replied. "But he's an archaeologist— a new kind of scientist—and for a scientist, *not* finding something can be just as important as finding it. For your Papa, the purpose of the expedition is to increase our knowledge of how people lived in the past. If he doesn't find what he's looking for, he will know to search some-where else."

"I just don't want him to be disappointed," Lulu said.

"He won't be," Vi said reassuringly.

Vi and her stepdaughter continued the packing, and soon they were joined by Gracie, Lulu's eight-year-old sister, and Miss Moran, the family's housekeeper. As they all worked, the dining room gradually regained something of its usual tidy appearance. The table, at least, was cleared of clothes, as the suitcases were filled to their brims, closed, locked, and secured with strong leather straps. Miss Moran then bustled off to prepare lunch, and Vi and the girls set about putting an assortment of books in a small trunk— schoolbooks for the spring term that Lulu and Gracie would miss at their school.

Checking the little timepiece pinned to her blouse, Vi said, "Your Papa and Max should be returning any minute now, and they will have Max's books and assignments. Then we can close this trunk." She looked about the room, and a pleased smile brought out her dimple. "We've made a lot of progress this morning, girls," she said.

"What about those shovels and paint brushes?" Gracie asked, pointing to the tumble of utensils on a chair in the corner. "Why are we taking these things anyway?"

"Those are your father's tools of the trade," Vi explained, "just as a carpenter has his hammer and nails. Each digging implement and each brush has a special purpose. I think we should let him pack those himself, so he will know where they are when he needs them."

"Quite right," came a deep voice from the entryway, and Mark Raymond entered, with fourteen-year-old Max just behind him. Max was carrying a heavy load of books, and Lulu went to help him. Gracie bounded to her father and received a warm hug.

"I'll let you help me with my tools," Mark told Gracie, "and I will tell you what each is used for."

Crossing the room, Mark gave Vi, his wife of more than a year, a kiss on the cheek and lovingly brushed that stray strand of hair back from her upturned face.

"When are your mother and Zoe coming?" he asked.

"About two o'clock," Vi said. "Mother's note said that Ed is bringing them. They will go to Samaritan House first and get Mrs. O'Flaherty. Oh, Mark, I can hardly believe that the time for our departure is so close. In two days we will be out on the ocean, on our way to the Christiana Islands." Her mouth breaking into its dimpled smile, she asked, "Do you have any idea how excited the children and I are?"

"Excited?" Mark replied in a teasing tone. "Max, Lulu, are you excited?"

Both children nodded their heads vigorously.

"And you too, Gracie?" he inquired of his youngest child.

Clapping her hands, Gracie beamed and exclaimed, "More than I've ever been in my whole life!"

"Well, I am excited as well," Mark said, "because you are all going to share this adventure with me. I am blessed, my dears, truly blessed to have you as my companions on this journey. Not every wife and child would be so happy to leave the comforts of home and hearth and travel to distant places," he added with a grin.

"But we are, Papa!" Lulu declared.

"I know you are," Mark said. He surveyed his children, his intense, blue-gray eyes lingering on each face for several moments and at last coming to his wife. "Dear Father in Heaven, You have blessed me with this family, and they are my strength," he said in a voice that betrayed the powerful emotion he felt. "Watch over us, Lord, as we embark on our new journey."

"And Lord, please help Papa find the treasure he's looking for," Lulu whispered, not even realizing that she had voiced her little prayer.

"The Lord has already led me to the real treasure in life," Mark said almost as softly as Lulu had spoken. "It is you, my dears. It is all of you."

After a moment, Mark spoke again in his normal tone: "Let's get back to work. We still have much to do, and these things aren't going to pack themselves!"

With the assistance of Miss Moran and Kaki Kennon, the genial young Irish maid who managed the housework with smooth efficiency, most of the packing was completed by the time Vi's family and Mrs. O'Flaherty arrived. Vi was re-pinning her hair at the mirror in the entry hall when she heard the sound of carriage wheels crunching over the gravel in the driveway. The children, dressed in their winter coats, caps, and mittens, were already waiting on the porch. Tossing a woolen shawl around her shoulders, Vi rushed out to join them, as her mother's carriage, with her big brother holding the reins, came to a stop.

Jumping down from the driver's seat, Ed Travilla helped his mother, Elsie, from the carriage and then lifted his young wife—Zoe Love Travilla—to the ground. The last passenger to receive his hand was Mrs. Maurene O'Flaherty, Vi's dear friend who would accompany the Raymonds on their trip to the Caribbean.

With much laughter and chatter, they all went inside, and Mark emerged from his study to greet them and take their coats.

"Thank goodness for your mother's large carriage," Mrs. O'Flaherty said to Vi. "I have a small trunk, a suitcase, and a valise—not too much, but still more than I could have brought in the buggy."

Mark and Max went to fetch Mrs. O'Flaherty's luggage but soon rejoined the others, who had settled around the fire blazing in the living room fireplace.

Zoe sat in a stuffed chair, which seemed almost to swallow her tiny frame, and Ed sat beside her, on the arm of the chair. "It's so marvelous to think that a week from now, you will have traded this February cold for sunshine and summer dresses," Zoe said to Vi. "There's no danger of storms, is there? I have been reading about the hurricanes in the Caribbean and the Gulf of Mexico."

"Very little danger," Vi replied. "Mark and Dr. Hockingham planned the trip for the time of year most conducive to their work and safety."

A relieved smile lit up Zoe's lovely heart-shaped face. "I wanted to be sure," she said. "You will be meeting Dr. Hockingham in Christiana?"

"Yes. It seemed easier that way," Vi said. "He is bringing two of his assistants and an artist, and they will arrive a few days before us."

"An artist?" Ed questioned. "Why is an artist needed on an archaeological expedition?"

"It's essential," Mark said, "that we have someone to make a detailed graphic record of each find. Even a small shard of pottery can be a clue to a people's culture. The artist will draw and paint images of anything we discover and also make precise measurements. We will all keep records, of course."

"Someday, you will be able to keep such records with photographs," Zoe suggested.

"That is already being done by a few scholars," Mark said, "but I think we will always need artists. Our Mr. Bottoms has great knowledge of artifacts, and I doubt any camera could duplicate his skills."

"Speaking of artists," Elsie Travilla said, "I received a letter yesterday from Philadelphia. Vi, your elder sister and her new baby girl are doing very well, as are young Benjamin and Lester, the proud father. According to Missy, Lester has just received a very prestigious commission. He has been engaged to paint the official portrait of the governor of Pennsylvania."

"Oh, I'm so pleased," Vi said. "It won't be long, I suspect, before that name of Lester Leland is as well known in this country for the artistry of his portraiture as those of Mr. Gilbert Stuart and Mr. John Singer Sargent. And I shall be very proud to say that he was my first teacher."

The conversation continued in this vein for some time, as they discussed various family members and friends, all of whom sent their love and best wishes to the Raymonds. Then Gracie asked, "Will you come to see us at the ship, Grandmamma Elsie?"

"Of course, my darling," Elsie said, "I will be there, and Ed and Zoe. Rosemary and Danny too. Your great-grandparents will come, and if the weather is not too cold, your Cousin Virginia Conley and her young Betsy will accompany them. We would not miss the chance to wish you *bon voyage*."

Gracie snuggled close to Elsie and said, "I'll miss you. I'm gonna bring you back a present from the island. Polly Appleton—she's my best-est friend, you know—wants a coconut. What would you like, Grandmamma?"

"Oh, dear, I've never been to an island like Christiana, so I don't know," Elsie replied, holding the little girl close. "I want you to pick something that you think I would enjoy. Will you do that?"

"Yes, ma'am," Gracie said. "Max and Lulu will help me find something very special for you."

The talk then turned to Samaritan House, the city mission that served the poor district of Wildwood. Vi and Mrs. O'Flaherty had founded the mission, and Mrs. O'Flaherty had been managing the place since Vi and Mark's marriage, though Vi remained very involved in its operation. Leaving the mission for months had been her one reservation about traveling to the Caribbean. But that problem had been resolved when Dr. David Bowman and his wife, Emily, who ran the mission's clinic together, volunteered to take over during Vi and Mrs. O'Flaherty's absence.

"With the doctor and Emily living at the mission, I can leave without the slightest qualm," Mrs. O'Flaherty said. "Why, Samaritan House practically runs itself now. When I think how inexperienced we were, Vi girl, when we first opened our doors to our neighbors—well, God provided for us. First Enoch and Christine Reeve, then Mary Appleton and Emily Clayton, then the doctor and Mr. Fredericks, who started our school, and so many dedicated volunteers... God must have wanted the mission to succeed, for He led each of us down very different paths to arrive at the same place."

"And you feel as confident as Maurene does?" Elsie asked Vi.

"Every bit as confident," Vi said. With a little blush, she added, "I would be vain indeed to think that Samaritan House could not get along without me for four months."

Miss Moran and Kaki brought tea for the adults and hot chocolate for the children. Everyone enjoyed their warm drinks and the conversation, until Ed stood and said, "We could easily while away the afternoon with pleasantry, but we came to work! You must have some tasks left for us."

Mark set his teacup on a table and said, "I do, Ed. There's a large wooden box in my study that needs filling with the camping gear and my maps and books. I could use a hand from you and Max."

"And I could use some sage advice from Mamma and Zoe," Vi said. "The girls and I have been trying to choose the dresses we should take. We aren't sure which we may need or how many."

Zoe almost jumped from her chair. "Well, if there's one thing I know, it's dresses," she bubbled. Reaching out to Lulu and Gracie, each of whom took one of her delicate hands, Zoe said, "Lead me to your closets, girls."

As they looked through the wardrobes in the upstairs bedrooms, Zoe and Elsie were indeed very helpful. Vi had already laid out a number of lightweight daytime dresses for herself, Lulu, and Gracie. Elsie assisted the girls to choose several dresses appropriate for church services, and then Zoe insisted that they each include a couple of fancy party dresses.

"You too, Vi. You will be important guests on the island," Zoe said. "I have done my research. Christiana is the main island of the Christiana Islands group. It is a British territory, and it has an English governor—Sir something or other. I forget his name. You will be staying in the capital city of Georgetown. The governor lives there and the American consul as well. The consul is the official representative of the United States to the islands, and I am sure you will meet him. My dear Papa was an American diplomat for many years, and he taught me how important it is to be prepared for anything. You have to be prepared if the consul asks you to tea or the governor invites you to dinner, don't you?"

The idea of dining with the governor intrigued Lulu, and she asked if his house might be a palace.

"I doubt it is so grand," Zoe said, tossing her blonde curls. "But it will probably be the nicest house on the island, with lots of servants. Governors often have many luxuries that the people they govern cannot afford," Zoe added with a little twist of her lips.

Lulu wondered what Zoe meant by this last remark. But Zoe was already instructing the girls to pack their party shoes and reminding them how important it was to include broad-brimmed hats to protect their skin from the tropical sun and asking if they had swimming costumes.

"Do you have a swimming dress?" Zoe asked Vi.

"I do," Vi said, "though since it is made of wool and covers me from neck to ankle, I fear it will sink me if I try to swim. I have something else to show you and Mamma. Some outfits that Alma Hansen made especially for me and the girls. I think you will find them quite—ah—quite revolutionary. Come and see."

Getting Ready for a Voyage

Their curiosity aroused, Elsie and Zoe followed Vi to the spare bedroom, where two large, rectangular clothing trunks stood upright and open on the floor. They looked like small clothing cupboards, with the family's clothes hanging from metal rods inside. Vi removed a buff-colored suit from one of the trunks. It consisted of a jacket and a skirt, very plain in design. Zoe could see that the jacket was looser than the current style and the skirt appeared shorter than normal. It was not, to Zoe's eyes, at all fashionable, and she looked at Vi in bewilderment.

"I call it my 'expedition outfit,' and the girls have similar suits," Vi said. "Though we will not be members of Mark's team, he has assured us that we will visit the dig site once the men have established their camp. With these clothes, we will be able to dress appropriately for a trip through the island's forested terrain."

"Well, dear, it certainly looks comfortable," Elsie commented. "What is this fabric?" she asked, feeling the sleeve of the jacket.

"It's called *khaki*," Vi said. "Khaki is a sturdy cotton material often used for military uniforms. In India, the word *khaki* means the color of dust."

"Isn't the skirt rather short?" Zoe asked, studying the outfit closely.

Vi smiled and said, "It isn't really a skirt at all." She held the garment at her waist and lifted aside the panel of fabric that gave it the appearance of a skirt. Beneath the panel were pants made of the same sturdy khaki! The pants were long enough to just cover Vi's knees.

"See," Vi said happily. "It looks like a proper skirt, but the panel wraps around from the back to the front and buttons on one side, concealing the pants beneath. The whole

13

thing is hemmed to come to the top of my high walking boots. Alma did the design, and she took every practicality and propriety into account. What do you think?"

"I think it's splendid," Elsie said as she examined the garment. "It's as practical as the clothing of our menfolk, though no one would ever mistake this charming outfit for male attire. Where did you and Alma get such an idea?"

"From Max's bicycle," Lulu said. "When Max got his bicycle last summer, I tried to ride it and so did Mamma. But our skirts and petticoats got all tangled up, and we couldn't peddle or anything. Papa said Mamma looked liked a powder puff on wheels, the way she was trying to hold her skirts up, and Mamma said how unfortunate it was that girls couldn't enjoy the healthy activity of riding a bicycle just because of our skirts."

"I was complaining about the situation one day when I was having a fitting at Alma's dress shop," Vi said, "and my complaints must have inspired her, because she created the design, basing it on the split-skirts some younger girls wear to ride horseback. When I told her about our trip to the tropics, she made this outfit for me, and two more for the girls."

Zoe exclaimed, "This could be a real trend! Just think how much easier it would be to ride a horse, as well as a bicycle. Personally I've never enjoyed riding side-saddle, because I always feel as if I'm about to slip off the horse's back. Of course, I'd prefer my riding skirt in a color other than that of dust—a heather blue, perhaps—and I'd like the jacket fitted at the waist, without those big pockets. But your outfit is perfect for tramping through the jungles or whatever exotic vegetation they have in Christiana. How very clever Alma is!"

"Then you don't think it's un-ladylike?" Vi asked.

"Not at all," Elsie said. "It's really quite feminine in cut and style. I should quite like a skirt like this for myself."

"What do you wear beneath it?" Zoe asked with a giggle.

"A cotton blouse, of course, with a chemise under the jacket," Vi replied. "And some very comfortable drawers beneath the skirt and pants. Alma thought of everything."

"And no petticoats," Lulu added with a bright grin that expressed her obvious satisfaction.

The large trunks were all closed and locked by the time the Travillas departed for Ion, as was the wooden box filled with Mark's tools, maps, and camping equipment. Elwood Hogg, the family's gardener, and his two strong brothers came the next morning to transport the heavy luggage to the docks of India Bay. There, the Raymonds' largest trunks and the box were loaded onto the steamship *Minerva* and stored in the ship's cargo hold for the voyage to Christiana.

The family spent the next morning completing the packing of their travel cases, and the children said good-bye to their friends on College Street. Then Mark left to meet with his faculty members at India Bay University, where he was head of the classical languages department and was also in the process of establishing the school's new department of archaeology. Meanwhile, Vi, Mrs. O'Flaherty, and the children paid a parting visit to their friends at Samaritan House. It was not a sad occasion for the adults, because the mission residents were almost as excited about the Raymonds' great adventure as were the Raymonds themselves.

Dr. Bowman and his wife, Emily, had a going-away present for Vi—a metal box full of medical supplies. "I pray that you won't need anything in this kit," the doctor said, "but safe is always better than sorry. Just be sure to keep taking those quinine pills. I know they are bitter, but they'll protect you against malarial fevers. I have included a prescription for more quinine, and I am sure there will be a chemist on the island to provide any medications you may need."

Old Widow Amos, who was one of the mission's most frequent and welcome visitors, had some words of advice for the children. "Now, you look out for each other down on that island. And watch for snakes and them dragon things I seen in my grandboy's picture magazines," she told them. "The magazines say those things are lizards, but they don't look like no lizards I ever saw."

Jacob Reeve, the four-year-old son of the mission's housekeeper and caretaker, had tears in his large brown eyes when he took Lulu's hand and said, "I wish you didn't have to go away. Will you write me a letter? Mama can read it to me." Lulu, who was not an overly sentimental girl, nevertheless felt the sting of tears when she hugged and kissed her little friend and promised to write him as often as she could.

But the hardest of all the leave-takings was between Gracie and Polly Appleton. The two girls had been friends almost from the moment Gracie first arrived in India Bay, and hardly a day went by that they didn't see each other. They went to the same school, for Vi had seen to it that Polly could attend Miss Broadbent's Female Academy, where Gracie and Lulu were students. (Susan Broadbent, the headmistress, had welcomed Polly to the school, and Polly was proving to be one her brightest and most creative students.)

"You've got all your books and lessons?" Polly asked. When Gracie replied that she had everything, Polly said in her grave way, "It's real important that you keep up, so we'll get promoted together."

"I know," Gracie said with equal seriousness, "and I'll keep up. We'll be in the same class next year. You won't forget me, will you? Four months is a very long time, and you might find other friends."

"How could I forget my best-est friend in the world?" Polly answered. She took Gracie's hand and squeezed it. "Four months isn't so very long," she said. "And just think, you get to miss the rest of the cold weather here. When you get back, it will be summer, and then we'll have the most wonderful time ever."

Polly finally allowed herself to smile, and her smile made Gracie respond in kind. Polly said, "Even when you're not here, you're in my heart all the time. Jesus will be watching over us both, remember, so we'll never be apart really. Not even when you're on that island and I'm in India Bay."

The girls were in Polly's room, and Polly went to her dresser. From the top drawer, she removed an envelope. "This is for you, but you can't open it till you're out at sea," she said softly. "It's my first letter to you, and you have to answer it as soon as you get to Christiana. You tell me what it's like there, and I'll write and tell you what's happening here."

Gracie took the envelope and looked at it. Then she laughed. Polly had written the address:

> Miss Grace Raymond
> Steamship Minerva
> Atlantic Ocean
> Planet Earth
> God's Kingdom

"I put my address on the back," Polly said, "so you won't forget it."

"I won't forget," Gracie said.

A masculine voice called from the kitchen.

"That's Dr. Bowman," Polly said. "I guess it's time for you to go. I won't cry if you won't."

"And I won't cry if you won't," Gracie giggled. Even so, two large tears overflowed her blue eyes and ran down her rosy cheeks.

"That's okay," Polly said, putting her arm around her friend's waist. "In Psalm 126, it says, 'Those who sow in tears will reap with songs of joy.' We'll do lots and lots of joyful singing when you come home."

CHAPTER

2

Memories of Other Times

Remember the wonders he has done....

1 CHRONICLES 16:12

*A*s hard as she tried, Lulu could not get to sleep. She even tried counting sheep, but the sheep kept turning into palm trees and colorful parrots and all the amazing things she imagined whenever she thought about the islands.

At last she gave up and relit her lamp. The clock on the mantel said it was almost eleven o'clock; in less than ten hours, she, her family, and Mrs. O'Flaherty would be on board the *Minerva*, and the ship would be steaming its way southward, following the Atlantic coastline toward the warm waters of the Caribbean. How could anyone sleep with such a journey on the horizon? It would be months before she could sleep in her own bed, in her own house, again, but Lulu hadn't felt even the smallest pang of regret. Going to the Christiana Islands was the adventure she had always longed for. What would they find there? What would the people be like? Would Georgetown be anything like India Bay?

Lulu sighed heavily. Her busy imagination simply wouldn't give her rest, so she decided to occupy her mind by writing in her journal. It lay on the bedside table, next to her Bible. She wrapped her thick robe around her shoulders and tucked her comforter about herself to keep out the night chill. Then she took up the journal, a gift from Vi's cousin Molly Embury, who was a real author and lived in Louisiana. Rummaging among the things on the tabletop, Lulu found her pencil. Before opening the journal, however, she ran her hand over its flower-patterned cloth cover. The flowers, so bright when Lulu had received the book, looked faded now, and the cloth was thin and frayed in places. There was a small tear on the back cover, caused when Lulu caught the book on a broken branch in her hidey-hole, but patched by Kaki. Far from being troubled by the somewhat tattered state of her journal, however, Lulu thought that its worn appearance reflected how much it was used, which would please Cousin Molly.

"A journal is like a private place for your thoughts," Molly had said in the card attached to her gift. "There is no right or wrong thing to write here. Keeping a journal is not an obligation; it is an *opportunity* to express yourself to your-self and, in my experience, to the Lord. So write about what you want, dear Lulu—your hopes, your fears, your dreams, your prayers—and write when you want."

Lulu turned to a clean page and was just about to press her pencil to the paper. But no words came to her. All of a sudden, she was unsure what to write about. She'd planned to record her thoughts about the exciting adventure ahead, but she realized that she really didn't know what might be ahead. She had been imagining the trip for so long, but now that the time had come…

Lulu felt a twinge of something uncomfortable, a lit-tle shiver of doubt or anxiety. The feeling passed almost as quickly as it had come, and she wanted to forget it. But that uncomfortable moment had taken away her desire to write. Instead of beginning a new entry, Lulu turned back to the front page of the journal. Her first entry was dated in December of 1884, a little more than a year earlier. Lulu noticed how different her handwriting was then. The letters looked so large and loopy. She remembered how hard she had worked on that first entry, and she began to read:

Yesterday my Papa married Miss Vi at her house at Ion. Miss Vi is now officially our new Mamma, and I am so happy. I never saw anyone so beautiful. She wore a white satin dress and carried a big bouquet of white roses. She had blue violets pinned in her hair and a white veil with lace on it. The violets were from her poor, dead father's hothouse. I could see that it made ~~Miss Vi~~ Mamma happy to have something of her father's with her. Papa looked very handsome in his new suit. Gracie and I got new dresses too. Mine is blue and Gracie's is pink. Miss Zoe and Rosemary were the bridesmaids, and their dresses were a kind of red color that Grandmamma Elsie calls maroon.

Mr. Horace Dinsmore, our new great-grandfather, brought Miss Vi to the altar. Uncle Ed stood up with Papa and held the wedding ring. Then Papa gave our new Mamma her ring, and right after that, the minister said they were husband and wife, and he prayed a special prayer for Papa and Mamma and our new family. That's what made it official, I guess.

There was a big party afterwards, and so many people were there. I know most of their names now, so I didn't make too many mistakes. We stayed at Ion overnight, and this morning we came back to our house, which is now our new Mamma's house too. Tomorrow, there's going to be a party at Samaritan House for the people in Wildwood.

Then Papa and Mamma are going on a trip. Mrs. O'Flaherty says the trip is a honeymoon, but she doesn't know why it's called that. Papa and Mamma are going to visit New Orleans. They will be gone for three weeks, and that's all right with us, because we want them to have a good time. Max and Gracie and me are going back to stay at Ion until Papa and Mamma return, and that will be fun for us. But I know that I'm going to miss Papa and my new Mamma. I love them both so much. I'm glad their wedding was the first one I ever went to, because it was so very splendid.

Lulu was amused by her own simple words. Reading the entry brought back a flood of warm memories of her parents' wedding and what was, Lulu now understood, the beginning of a new life for all of them.

She turned the pages of the journal and stopped to read an entry that began, "I WON THE POETRY WRITING CONTEST TODAY!!!" It had been what Mrs. O'Flaherty called a red letter day. It was in May of 1885—Lulu's first year in her new school—and Lulu clearly recalled how she had felt when she wrote this entry:

I WON THE POETRY WRITING CONTEST TODAY!!! I wrote a poem about my special place under the boxwood bush, and my teacher decided it was the best of anybody's! I hope I'm not guilty of pride, but I can't help feeling really good. I didn't even like reading poetry at first, because I enjoy stories so much, but Mamma told me that poems are stories written in a different way. With Mamma helping me, I have worked very hard to understand poetry better, and I guess this proves that all my hard work was worth it.

Miss Zoe has also been very kind to me. I wasn't sure that I would like the Female Academy, though Miss Broadbent is the kindest headmistress and the teachers are just as nice. But I wasn't sure if I would be a good student, and I was scared that I couldn't make friends. Then Miss Zoe, who teaches French and Italian to the older girls, helped me. She doesn't treat me any different from the other girls at school, so I'm not a teacher's pet. But she said she'd be my tutor, just as Great-grandpapa Horace was her tutor. I didn't need a lot of help in arithmetic and science, which are my best subjects, and I love to read, so I do well in literature, especially now that I really enjoy poetry. But my history wasn't so good, and Miss Zoe taught me all about how this country was founded and what has happened since it became the United States. She helps me with my spelling too. She says it is not enough to spell a word right, so I've leaned to use the dictionary. I find out what every new spelling word means and how to pronounce it and how to use it. That way, I understand the words.

Papa is always willing to help me with history and some other subjects. I'm glad he didn't go on an expedition this year, because he has taken lots of his time to help me and Max and Gracie get used to our new schools. But he will go away again next year, and I am hoping maybe he'll take us with him. I really want to go with him sometime, dear Jesus, if that's what You want for us.

Lulu smiled at these last words. *Thank You, Jesus*, she thought, *for answering my prayer and making my dream come true. Thank You for letting us have this adventure together. Please take care of us, Lord, and help me and Gracie and Max be the best children for our Papa and Mamma. And help me not be scared or*

sick when we're out on the ocean. This is my first trip on a ship, You know, and I want it to be exciting.

She flipped through some more pages and stopped to read an entry for another memorable day, this one dated in July of 1885:

As of this very day, Miss Zoe is my Aunt Zoe, and she was the prettiest bride ever, except for our Mamma, of course. Miss Alma made her dress, but Aunt Zoe ordered all the silk and lace and pearl buttons from Paris, France, which I should like to visit when I am older. Her veil was made from some very old and delicate lace that had belonged to her mother. She had a necklace and earrings made with real sapphires that are almost exactly the color of her eyes. Those were a gift from Uncle Ed.

Mamma was the matron of honor, which is what a married lady is called when she's the main attendant at a wedding. Papa was Uncle Ed's best man, and Great-grandpapa Horace gave Miss Zoe away. It was very sweet. The minister asked, "Who gives this woman in holy matrimony?" And Great-grandpapa said, "My wife, Rose, and I do, in the name of her late mother and father."

The wedding was at The Oaks, which was decorated like a place in a beautiful dream, and we all had lunch at great long tables outside on the lawn. There were even more people at this wedding than at Papa and Mamma's. Lots of the family came, like Aunt Missy and Uncle Lester from Philadelphia. Cousin Molly and Mr. Embury came from Louisiana with their daughters and little boy. So did Cousin Isa Conley Keith and her husband, Reverend Keith, and

their children. I also met some interesting guests who
are not family. Especially Reverend and Mrs.
Carpenter from New Orleans, where they have a big
mission and school for the poor—like Samaritan
House, I imagine. Mrs. Carpenter is Aunt Chloe's
granddaughter, and they had a wonderful visit. Aunt
Chloe wasn't very well during the winter, but
Grandmamma Elsie says that seeing all the Carpenters
is the best medicine in the world.

I also met a real ambassador! His name is Monsieur
Lecroix, and he's the French ambassador to our government in Washington. He's an old friend of Mamma
and Aunt Zoe and Uncle Ed and Mrs. O. He came
with his wife, who is lovely and so nice. Zoe told me, <u>in
strict confidence</u>, that Monsieur is really a Duke but
he tells no one because he does not believe in high titles
that set one person above others. I thought that was
very interesting. It's an idea I want to think more
about. Aunt Zoe also told me that she won't be teaching at the Female Academy next year, which is sad for
me, but she will teach at the school at Ion. I could see
how happy that makes her, so it makes me happy too.

Mrs. O says that for a girl who never went to any
weddings in her life, I am quickly making up ground.
Aunt Zoe and Uncle Ed's wedding was the third wedding I've attended. The second was when Miss Emily
married Dr. Bowman. Their wedding was at
Samaritan House, and it wasn't nearly as fancy as
Aunt Zoe and Uncle Ed's wedding. But it was so much
fun! At the party after the service, there was wonderful food and then <u>hours</u> of music and dancing and
singing. Mrs. O said it reminded her of the country

weddings she went to when she was a girl in Ireland. Dr. Bowman told me that he and Miss Emily are going to live in Wildwood and that they hope to open a real hospital there. Wouldn't that be wonderful?

Lulu read the rest of this entry and then turned several pages, stopping at one dated in October of 1885. She drew her robe closer around her as she read:

Please help me, Dear Lord, to be strong for Mamma tomorrow. I know that she is sad because her great-grandfather, Mr. Dinsmore, Sr., has died, even though he was very old and had been very ill for a long time. He is with You now, and that makes Mamma happy, but still, it will be hard for her and all her family to say good-bye to him at the funeral. I only met him a few times, but he seemed a good and kind man. Our Great-grandpapa Horace has told us stories about his father and what it was like to grow up at Roselands, and I wish I could have known old Mr. Dinsmore better. I do know that Mamma loved him very much, and she will miss him. So help me, Lord, and help Max and Gracie and Papa to do whatever we can to help Mamma and Grandmamma Elsie and everyone else. I remember how terrible and lonely I felt when my own dear first Mamma died, but that was before I understood Your saving grace and how we will all be together again someday, living with You in Heaven. I just want to do what's right tomorrow for Mamma Vi's sake.

Lulu stopped reading. Slowly, she closed the journal and laid it aside, as she thought back to the day of Mr.

Horace Dinsmore, Sr.'s funeral. It had not been such a sad day after all, she remembered. The sun was shining, and the trees were near the height of their autumn color. The burial had been at Roselands, in the Dinsmore family cemetery, and then the family and their friends had gathered in the house. People began to talk about Mr. Dinsmore and all that he'd done in his more than ninety years of life. Some of the family stories were very funny, and no one hesitated to laugh. That had surprised Lulu, but it also made her feel good in a way she didn't quite understand.

When Lulu asked Vi about it, a week or so after the funeral, Vi had said, "It would make my great-grandfather happy that you enjoyed those stories. He would not want us to weep at his passing. His life was long and full, Lulu. He endured many losses when he was younger—two wives, two of his three sons, my own father, Edward, who was as close to him as a son—but his suffering finally brought him to the Lord, and he found peace in his heart. That is what we were celebrating, Lulu, and I think that is what gave you good feelings. My great-grandfather knew the peace of God's love here on earth, and now he is enfolded in God's love for all eternity. For a Christian, it is possible to feel great sadness and grief at the loss of someone we love, yet at the same time feel immense joy that our loved one has at last embarked on the most glorious journey of all, going home to our Heavenly Father. It can be confusing, this mix of feelings, of grief and joy."

"It is confusing," Lulu had responded. "Just the idea of someone I love dying is so scary. I lost my sweet mother, and I don't ever want to lose anybody else ever again."

"But when anyone who loves the Lord leaves us, it is the fulfillment of God's promise to us, the promise of eternal life with Him," Vi said gently. "No one who believes in Him is ever lost to you, my darling. Do you remember the story we read together of Jairus, the synagogue ruler, in the Gospel of Mark? Jairus was with Jesus when he was told that his daughter had died. Do you recall what Jesus said to Jairus?"

Lulu thought for a moment; then she replied, "Yes, ma'am. Jesus said, 'Don't be afraid; just believe.' And they went to the man's house, and everybody told Jesus that the girl was dead. But Jesus said she was asleep. He took her hand and told her to get up, and she did!"

Vi smiled, placed her arm around Lulu, and embraced her warmly: "If you keep the Lord's words in your heart, my dearest, they will get you through times when you feel scared that you might lose someone you love. If you believe, Jesus will give you the strength to bear whatever may happen."

"Do you ever feel scared that way?" Lulu asked.

A strange, distant look came to Vi's eyes. Lulu saw it, but she didn't know what her stepmother was thinking — she couldn't know that Vi was remembering a stormy summer day when the same girl she was holding close now was nearly lost to her. Vi could almost see the flashes of lightning and hear the booming thunderclaps. Goosebumps rose on Vi's arms as she recalled her fear and dread.

"Yes, Lulu, I have felt that scared," Vi said softly. "But I had Jesus' words in my heart — 'Don't be afraid, just believe.' When I was most afraid, I turned my fears over to Him, and He led me along the right path."

Thinking back on this conversation, Lulu still wondered what scary experience Vi had been talking about. Maybe she would find out someday, but at this moment, Lulu was too drowsy to speculate. She had intended to write in her journal, but her eyelids were heavy now, and she could barely keep them open. She shook herself, rousing just long enough to turn out her lamp. Then she rolled over in bed, lying on her side and snuggling deep beneath the warm blankets. She was sound asleep when her journal slid off the comforter. She didn't hear the sharp smack when it fell to the floor.

Bump, thump, thud—a series of loud sounds woke Lulu, and in her sudden waking, she wondered if the house were falling in. Then she heard a shout—"Gracie!"—followed by hurried footsteps outside her door.

Throwing back her covers, Lulu hopped out of her bed and ran out her door and into the hallway. She caught a quick glimpse of her father's head before it disappeared below the banister. She rushed to the top of the staircase and looked down to see Mark bending over Gracie, who was sitting on the floor and howling. An open travel valise lay beside her, its contents spilled higgledy-piggledy around her.

"Are you hurt?" Mark was asking his youngest child urgently.

"No, Papa," Gracie managed to say between sobs. "I—I—I tripped on the carpet! But look—look at Evalina!" Gracie pointed a shaking finger at something near the valise. "She's broken to bits!"

This brought on a fresh rush of tears. Mark, seeing that his little girl was not injured, reached for the object of her concern. From her perch at the top of the stairs, Lulu could see that it was Gracie's favorite doll, a pretty thing with porcelain head, arms, and legs.

"Look at her head!" Gracie wailed. "She's all cracked! And her nose has come off! Where's Evalina's nose?"

Mark searched through the scattered items around the valise and found a small piece of china. "Hush now," he said. "Here's her nose. It's a clean break, and it and the cracks can be repaired, Gracie. Unlike little girls, Evalina can be repaired with some glue."

"But she'll never be the same, Papa," Gracie whimpered.

"Maybe not," Mark replied, lifting Gracie to her feet. "Maybe she'll be even better. But why did you bring that heavy valise down by yourself? I told you I would carry it."

Gracie hung her head and said something that Lulu, from her vantage point at the top of the stairs, couldn't understand.

"Luckily you weren't hurt," Mark said with a hint of sternness. "I want you to use your common sense, Gracie. I understand how eager you are to begin our trip, but you knew that case was too heavy for you to lift. If you had just waited a few more minutes, I could have carried it, and this accident to Evalina wouldn't have happened."

"I'm sorry, Papa," Gracie said, raising her forlorn little face to him.

"I know you are, darling," Mark responded, running his hand gently over her curls. "Now, let's go get your breakfast. We'll ask your Mamma and Miss Moran if they know of a good doll doctor."

"Are there such things?" Gracie asked curiously.

"I'm sure there must be," Mark said. He was still holding the doll and the little piece of its nose in one hand. "I doubt that Evalina is the first doll to suffer such an injury."

As Lulu watched, her father and sister walked toward the kitchen.

"What was that racket?" Max asked, coming up behind Lulu and looking over her shoulder.

"Gracie fell on the steps," Lulu answered. Stiffling a yawn, she added, "Gracie's not hurt, but Evalina's got a broken nose. Papa's taking care of everything."

"Hey, you better get dressed," Max said. "Didn't you hear Mamma call us to breakfast? Did you oversleep?"

"I guess so," Lulu said. "I was up late."

"Too excited to sleep, huh?" Max said, giving her a playful poke. "Me, too. Well, go get ready, and dress warmly. It's a clear day, but cold, and it'll be colder when we put out to sea."

Max started down the stairs, taking a couple of quick steps, then turned to look back at Lulu. "I never thought I'd be saying that—*put out to sea*." He was grinning almost from ear to ear.

Max continued downstairs, calling "Get a move on, slowpoke," over his shoulder.

An hour later, Vi was in the entry hall, counting the travel bags one last time, when Elwood Hogg brought the carriage to the front of the house.

"Now, don't you worry about anything," Miss Moran said. "We'll take good care of the house, and with Elwood staying here, we'll be safe and sound."

"You just write us now and then and let us know what's going on with you and Professor Raymond and the children. Gracious me, I'm already missing you folks and you haven't left the house yet," Kaki Kennon added with a laugh in her voice but a mist of tears in her eyes.

Vi hugged Kaki close. "Oh, I wish you were both going with us," she said with emotion.

Returning the hug, Kaki said lightly, "Well, Miz Vi, I had my one adventure on that ocean, when I came over from Ireland. All that tossing about on the waves... I never did get my — what did they call it? — my 'sea legs.' That's when I promised myself I'd keep solid ground under my feet forever after."

Vi stood back and smiled at the young maid. Despite her anticipation of the trip, it was very hard for Vi to leave these two women and her home on College Street and Samaritan House.

"No tears, now. No tears," Miss Moran chirped as she took her turn hugging Vi. "I'm old enough to tell you both that four months is not so very long. You'll be back before we know it, and, oh, what grand stories you'll have for us! Just promise to be careful of yourself, Miss Vi, and the family. I don't want to hear that you've been carried off by pirates or some such."

Vi tossed her head back and laughed. "I think the pirates are all gone now, Miss Moran. We'll have the British Navy to protect us in Christiana."

As Mark and Max loaded the last of the travel cases into the carriage, Mrs. O'Flaherty and the girls said their good-byes to Miss Moran and Kaki. Gracie tried her hardest not to cry, but when Miss Moran promised that Evalina would be made as good as new and would be waiting when the family returned, the youngest Raymond burst into tears.

"You are the good-est person," Gracie said, holding Miss Moran tightly about the waist.

"I trust you and Lulu and Max to be the best children for your Mamma and Papa," Miss Moran replied with a little difficulty, for she now had tears streaming from her eyes.

There was another round of hugs, kisses, and drying of tears, followed by a happy scramble as the family got into the carriage. Max climbed up into the driver's seat next to Elwood and surveyed his house and neighborhood one final time. He drew in a deep breath and thought he caught the scent of salt in the chill breeze.

"Out on the sea in ships," he said with a grin.

"What's that you said, Max?" asked Elwood.

"It's from one of the Psalms," Max said, and he quoted, " 'Others went out on the sea in ships; they were merchants on the mighty waters. They saw the works of the LORD, his wonderful deeds in the deep.' "

"You're gonna see some wondrous things yourself, down on them islands," Elwood said. "Yes, sir, I think you're gonna have a mighty wondrous time."

Cracking the reins, Elwood headed the buggy in the direction of the docks, where the seamen on the *Minerva* were busily readying the ship to weigh anchor for its next voyage.

About a dozen members of the Dinsmore and Travilla families were at the dock to bid them farewell with a sprinkling of tears and much excitement. When the *Minerva* at last steamed slowly away from its berth, its horns blaring, the Raymonds and Mrs. O'Flaherty stood on the deck and waved and waved until their loved ones were out of sight. Only after the shore was no longer visible did they realize

how biting the cold wind was, and they hurried inside to the warmth of the passenger lounge.

In their imaginations, the children expected to be at sea for a very long time, but in fact, the voyage took only a matter of several days. This was a great relief to Gracie, who never did quite get her "sea legs" in the rough waters of the Atlantic. But each day after the first, the weather grew warmer, and the ocean became calmer. By the time they reached the busy port of Havana, Cuba, where some of the passengers disembarked and cargo was loaded and unloaded, they had exchanged their winter clothes for summer garb. The day was as bright as the Fourth of July, and so were their spirits. The next morning they would reach Christiana, and the real adventure would begin.

CHAPTER

3

Arriving in
Georgetown

*I do not want to see you now and
make only a passing visit;
I hope to spend some time
with you, if the
Lord permits.*

1 CORINTHIANS 16:7

The waters off the port of Georgetown were too shallow for the great steamship, so it dropped anchor in the deep, and the Raymonds, Mrs. O'Flaherty, and their luggage were transferred to a smaller, much older boat. This boat ferried the family and a few other passengers the short distance to the island. After finding space on a bench on the boat's deck, Vi literally had to hold her three excited children down on their seats, as the vessel plowed toward the brilliant azure water that encircled the island. The sea was a little choppy, and the creaky old boat did not offer the smoothest ride.

"Just sit until we reach the shore," Vi said a little impatiently. Then she laughed and said, "I am not properly attired to dive into the sea and rescue a child who has fallen overboard. I want us all to be dry when we reach our destination."

"But I can hardly see anything from here," Gracie complained, wiggling under Vi's restraining hand.

"Then get up on my lap," Mrs. O said, "and you will have a clear view over the railing."

Mark soon joined them on the bench. "I shall be so glad when we are in our hotel and I do not have to count our bags and trunks and boxes again," he said with good humor. "I do not like this endless counting of luggage that always seems to come with travel. Well, children, what are your first impressions?"

"It's hot," Gracie said quickly, "like India Bay in the summer. And very bright. I like the way the sun feels, but the light makes me blink."

"The water is so blue and clear," Max commented. "It's hard to tell where the sea stops and the sky begins, for they are nearly the same color. That is because of the light, isn't it, Papa?"

"The light is one reason," Mark said. "The sandy shore of the island continues some distance under the water, and the water around the island is not very deep. The water appears light blue because the surface beneath the water reflects the color of the sky. The sea floor is much deeper, so the water appears to be a much darker blue. But if you dipped a glass into the sea and studied its contents, you'd see that the water is not blue at all."

Lulu didn't say anything, but she was drinking in all that she saw and felt as the ferryboat chugged its way toward shore—the heat, the light, the colors. She stared at the outline of the island against the clear blue sky. From a distance, it seemed like a dark, cone-shaped silhouette rising up from the sea like a mountain, coming to a ragged plateau somewhere in the distance.

"I thought the island would be flat," she said at last, "but it's not at all. It's shaped like the volcanoes in my science book."

"Excellent observation," Mark said. "The Christiana Islands were formed by volcanic activity many, many thousands of years ago. What you see is the top of what remains of the volcano. If we could see into the very top of that mountain, we would find a deep hole from which lava once flowed."

"What's lava?" Gracie asked, for she had not heard the word before.

"It's rock from deep inside the earth," Vi explained. "It becomes so hot that it melts and forces its way up through the ground. When we are settled in and begin our lessons, we will study the geology of this region and how volcanoes are formed."

"And how they explode," Max added mischievously.

Gracie's eyes widened.

"Don't worry, dearest," Vi said soothingly. "This volcano hasn't been active—hasn't exploded—in a very long time. We're quite safe."

The boat was nearing the wharf, and they could see people and low buildings. There seemed to be a great deal of activity. The wharf extended out into the water from a wall of stone that rose above the sandy beach. The stream-driven engine that powered the boat changed its sound, and they felt the vessel slowing. As it slowed, the boat bounced up and down in the breaker waves that were accompanying it to the beach, and Gracie, who had experienced several bouts of seasickness on the ocean voyage, said, "Uh-oh." But they were docking now, and as the bouncing subsided, so did Gracie's queasiness. Some men on the boat threw heavy ropes to more men on the wharf who used the ropes to maneuver the boat into its place alongside the wharf and secure it. The engine's noisy chugging stopped.

The family left the boat, walking by a wide gangplank onto the lower level of the wooden wharf. A set of stairs took them up to the main level, where they were engulfed by another kind of sea, this one made up of people. Mark was immediately surrounded by men offering to carry their luggage—"for just a few shillings, sir"—and arguing among themselves about who was the strongest and most honest. At the same time, Vi, Mrs. O'Flaherty, and the children were besieged by a crowd of native boys and girls loudly selling the wares they carried in baskets—fresh bananas, fans crafted of palm fronds, odds and ends of jewelry made from seashells. One enterprising lad carried a bucket and ladle and promised "fresh water, tastes so good, for the ladies and the young gentleman after your long journey. Please, missus, just one pence for all your pretty family." The boy's cheerful grin appealed to Vi, but she knew better than to drink water from an unknown source and said a firm, "No, but thank you."

The pushing of the sellers frightened Gracie, and she clung to Vi's skirts. Even Lulu was a little overwhelmed and grabbed Mrs. O'Flaherty's hand. Mark cast an exasperated glance at his wife and shouted, "Hockingham is supposed to meet us. But I don't see him!"

"Here I am, Mark!" came a deep, rich voice from the midst of the sellers.

Mark recognized the voice but could not see the man it belonged to.

"I'm coming!" the voice yelled. "Out of my way! Let me through! Ouch! That was my foot! Make way! Make way!"

Suddenly the yammering, jostling crowd parted, and like Moses through the Red Sea, a short man in a white linen suit and straw hat emerged.

"Shoo! Scat now! No sales here today," he called out to the local children, shaking his hands at them as if he were waving off a pesky litter of kittens.

Instantly, the island children scattered, while the men wanting to carry the luggage ceased their arguing and drifted away in disappointment. This struck Vi as a surprising thing, for by his appearance, Dr. Hockingham did not seem at all imposing. He was several inches shorter than Vi and rather round in face and girth. He had very little hair on his head but wore a thick moustache and neatly trimmed beard, which were auburn red peppered with gray. The top of his bald head and his nose and cheeks almost glowed red with sunburn. He looked, Vi thought, more like an elf or a gnome than a man capable of commanding a crowd to do his bidding.

"Good to have you here," Dr. Hockingham said to the new arrivals. "I've brought men and a cart to carry your luggage. How was your trip? No stormy weather, I hope."

As Mark replied to his friend and colleague, Vi understood why the young sellers and the baggage carriers had responded so promptly to this little man. It was his voice — deep, strong, resonant, and full of authority.

"We had a very pleasant voyage," Vi said as she shook hands with Dr. Hockingham. "It is so good to meet you at last. Mark speaks of you so often that I feel as if we were old acquaintances."

This brought a grin from Dr. Hockingham. "I, as well, feel as if we were long acquainted, Mrs. Raymond. I regret that I was unable to attend your wedding, for I knew you must be an exceptional young woman just by the changes you wrought in my friend Mark. When we were on our dig in Mexico, I recognized the light in his eyes and his smile. You did that, Mrs. Raymond."

Vi blushed at his compliment. She wasn't certain how to reply, so she quickly introduced Dr. Hockingham to Mrs. O'Flaherty and the children. Three men had come forward while they all chatted, and seeing them, Dr. Hockingham made another round of introductions.

"This is Thomas Barr," he began, and a tall, very dark man with penetrating brown eyes and strong, fine facial features stepped forward. "Thomas is our guide and the head man of our team," Dr. Hockingham explained.

The next to be introduced was Abraham Mercer, and the third man was named Liberty O'Dwyer.

"You are Irish, perhaps?" Mrs. O'Flaherty asked the last man.

"A little," Mr. O'Dwyer said with a sheepish look. "My great-grandfather was an Irish seaman, ma'am. We're all a mixed lot here—a bit of this and a bit of that. Irish, English, Scottish, Spanish, African, French, Portuguese, Dutch. Our ancestors came from the four points of the compass. But most of all, ma'am, we're islanders through and through."

"Well, it's good to meet an islander with a few leaves of Eire's emerald green in his family tree," Mrs. O'Flaherty replied with a wide smile. *And the Irish gift of gab too*, she thought to herself.

Mark greeted the men and shook their hands. Then Dr. Hockingham explained that the two young scholars who were also to be part of the team had been delayed but would join the expedition in another month. "Perhaps we will have found something by then, and we can put their youthful brawn to use at digging," the senior professor said with a hearty laugh.

Mark and the three native men went to collect the baggage and load the cart, while Dr. Hockingham directed the ladies and children to a waiting carriage. He would escort them to the hotel, and Mark and the men would follow in the cart.

As they rode through the town, Dr. Hockingham carried on a lively conversation, and the children peppered him with questions about the island and its history. But Vi's attention was distracted. The surroundings were so strange and intriguing. She was fascinated by the small, low, wood and stucco buildings that lined the dusty roadway. The buildings were mostly whitewashed and almost shimmered in the strong midday light, but their doors and shutters were painted in vibrant hues of red and blue and green and purple — a rainbow of colors that was repeated in the clothing of many of the women and children she saw, and in the fruits and vegetables heaped on the street vendors' barrows they passed. The scene made Vi think of villages on the Mediterranean coast of Italy. The sounds of the street were a mingling of shouting voices, laughter, and music that was entirely foreign to Vi's ears, yet also familiar in a way she couldn't quite explain to herself.

The carriage took them into a more prosperous neighborhood, where the road was paved in stones and the houses were larger, with iron balconies, and less colorfully decorated. Lush gardens were visible behind their protective fences and walls, and the sweet smells of the indigenous flora scented the air. The sounds were muted in comparison to the busy street market in the wharf area, but not even the rattling of the carriage wheels over stone could drown out the chirping and squawking and whistling of the birds.

Near the end of this street, Dr. Hockingham pointed out a house with a wrought iron fence and an American flag flying from an upstairs balcony. "That it where Mr. Bottoms and I are staying," he said. "It's the home of the United States consul. I do not usually get such elegant accommodations, but the consul is an old friend of mine, from our undergraduate days at Yale. He and his good wife are away right now, visiting family in New Hampshire, so Bottoms and I have the run of the place."

They turned a corner, and Vi saw they were in a business district with shops and office buildings. She realized that this must be in the center of the town, for it was a large square. In the center of the square was a smaller and less raucous version of the market at the wharfs, with a number of people selling from carts. Here and there, she saw groups of ladies in pastel dresses that would have been right at home on the main street of India Bay on a hot summer day. She also noticed a few soldiers in the uniform of the British Army and wondered whether they were on duty. On the opposite side of the square, partly obscured by clumps of tall palm trees, Vi spotted a white building with a square steeple.

The carriage drew to a halt before a long, two-story building trimmed in the kind of iron work she'd seen on some of the houses. The building's facade was painted a garish pinkish color, and the iron work was painted white. Sheer, white curtains fluttered from every window. It made Vi think of a birthday cake.

"Welcome to the Empire Hotel," Dr. Hockingham declared. "Personally, I call it the 'teacake,' because it reminds me of those fancy iced cakes my late wife would serve whenever she entertained the other faculty wives."

"I was thinking much the same thought," Vi said with a wry smile.

A man in fancy dress helped the travelers from the carriage, and Dr. Hockingham led them inside. While he and Vi tended to the registration, Mrs. O and the children looked around the long, large room that was hotel's lobby.

"I'm glad it isn't pink in here," Lulu said in a low tone. "I wouldn't want to live inside a pink teacake."

In fact, the hotel interior was quite comfortably furnished in tropical style, and all the rooms were painted a creamy white. Their second-floor bedrooms were spacious and airy, with glass doors opening onto small balconies and potted tropical plants flourishing in the corners. The furniture in each room was simple, but the beds were large, with good mattresses. Each bed was hung with drapes of a soft, thin netting, and Mrs. O explained that the nets would be spread around the beds at night to keep mosquitoes and other flying insects away from the sleepers. The floors were made of dark tiles, manufactured on the island, and the young Raymonds enjoyed the hollow sounds produced by walking on the tiles in their hard-soled shoes. There was no gaslight or electricity; each of the bedrooms had a single oil lamp but was well equipped with candles. (Vi said that the kind of oil suitable for lamps had to be imported and was very expensive.)

They had three bedrooms—one for Mark and Vi, one for Mrs. O'Flaherty, and one for the children. Max grumbled about sharing space with his little sisters, until Vi assured him that he would get his own room when Mark went on the expedition. "The hotel is nearly full with guests right now," Vi told him, "and I couldn't get a fourth room near the others. But when your father leaves, Mrs. O will move in with me, and you shall have her room to yourself. Will that suit you?" Max gladly agreed that he could put up with his sisters, as long as it wasn't for the entire four months of their stay.

Mark arrived just in time to join his family and Dr. Hockingham for lunch in the hotel dining room, and much of the conversation involved the men's plans. Dr. Hockingham had brought along several rough maps, which he laid out on the table for everyone to see. He pointed out Georgetown on the south of the island and then the expedition location at the base of the mountain on the north side of the island. "It's about two days' journey from here with the carts," he explained, "and relatively easy until we pass beyond the sugar cane plantations and enter the jungle."

"How do you know you're going to the right place?" Lulu asked.

"Ah, that's a very good question, young lady," Dr. Hockingham said. "Your Papa spent a good deal of his time studying the history of this island and also the maps that go back several centuries. He has pinpointed this area"—he jabbed at the map—"as the most likely site for the kind of evidence we seek. And I concur."

"We don't *know* that this will be the right place," Mark said. "We are making an educated guess based on careful study of the information we have."

"But if it's the wrong place, you'll waste a lot of time, won't you, Papa?" Max said.

"In one sense, you are right, my boy," Mark agreed. "We might lose time searching, but it won't be wasted time. Suppose that my supposition is mistaken and we find no evidence of ancient culture. We will nevertheless add to our knowledge, and the knowledge of our fellow scholars, by eliminating that area from our search. We will have new information that will be useful for future searches. And," he added with a grin, "we may not find what we seek, but there is always the chance we may find something equally interesting."

"That's quite true, children," Dr. Hockingham said. "The history of archaeology is filled with instances of people who went in search of one thing and found something else of equal or greater value."

"Then I hope you find both," Lulu declared firmly. "I hope you find what you are looking for and also something unexpected and just as important."

"The secret to doing that," Mark said, brushing Lulu's freckled nose playfully with his finger, "is to keep one's eyes and one's mind wide open to possibilities."

Mrs. O'Flaherty then asked what the terrain would be like in the exploration, and Mark and Dr. Hockingham described it as best they could without having been there. They knew that the site was in a wild, uncultivated area where just a few native people lived. "We believe that this part of the island was once the sea coast, but that it has been transformed into land by lava flows from eruptions of the volcano."

"Eruptions!" Gracie exclaimed. "But Mamma said there was no danger."

"Your Mamma is right. The volcano hasn't erupted for a long time," Mark said. "The last time, I believe, was almost three hundred years ago. It is dormant now. That means that it is sleeping quite peacefully, Gracie, so don't worry."

"I won't, Papa," the little girl said, adding in a low tone, "but I'm still gonna ask God not to wake up that old volcano anytime soon."

After lunch, Mark and Dr. Hockingham went off to attend to a number of tasks involved in preparing for their expedition. It was very hot outside, so Vi suggested that the children might want to read for a while and perhaps have a nap in their room. When the sun began to sink lower in the sky, she promised, they would take a walk and explore the town square. Though the children were anxious to see their new surroundings, they were all tired from the morning's activities and readily accepted Vi's suggestion.

After getting the children settled, Vi and Mrs. O'Flaherty went downstairs and adjourned to the veranda that ran along the entire length of the hotel's rear ground level, looking out to a garden surrounded by high stucco walls. The veranda was shaded beneath a canvas canopy.

The ladies said a polite hello to a couple of guests who were seated at a table and playing cards. Looking about, Vi spied some rocking chairs a bit apart from the card players, and she and Mrs. O'Flaherty occupied these.

"I really should finish the unpacking," Vi said, "but this spot is just too inviting."

"It is a charming setting," Mrs. O agreed. "I think we should follow the customs of the island—work hard in the early and late parts of the day, and rest when the sun is at its full power. It is a different way from what we are used to, but you know the saying: 'When in Rome, do as the Romans do.' Relax. There is plenty of time to unpack."

"I wonder what is happening at Samaritan House right now," Vi said several minutes later.

"Mary and Christine are making preparations for the afternoon meal, as usual, and Jacob is probably playing with Jam by the warm fire in the kitchen," Mrs. O'Flaherty responded. "David and Lucy are seeing patients in the clinic. Enoch may be checking the furnace or perhaps repairing that broken latch on the cellar door. Soon he will hitch the pony to the buggy and set out to collect young Polly at school. The children in the nursery are just waking from their naps, and some of our wonderful volunteers are preparing milk and biscuits for the little ones' afternoon treat. Don't you worry, Vi girl. The mission and your home are running smoothly, for you left them in good hands."

"I know," Vi replied. "Still—oh, you're right, Mrs. O. I have no cause to worry about what is happening there. It's just that I was reminded of Samaritan House and Wildwood today, when we drove through the shopping area around the wharf. At first, I couldn't think why it seemed familiar. Then I realized it was like a summer day in Wildwood, when people are on the street, darting in and out of the shops and stopping to chat with neighbors."

"Umm," said Mrs. O'Flaherty in a lazy way. "I have visited many places in my life, and I have observed that in spite of obvious differences, people are basically the same from place to place and culture to culture."

Vi was about to add a thought to the conversation, but at that moment, a young boy ran up to the ladies, his bare feet slapping softly on the tiled veranda floor. He stopped beside Vi's chair and said, "A letter for Mrs. Raymond."

He held out a small silver tray on which a white envelope lay. Vi took the letter, and the boy looked up at her with a shy smile. He hadn't been certain which of the two women was Mrs. Raymond, and he was very glad he hadn't made a mistake. Vi took a coin from her small purse, placed it on the tray, and thanked him. The boy's smile widened, and his eyes shone as he took the coin and bowed at the waist before hurrying back inside the hotel.

Vi opened the envelope and read the note it contained.

"We have an invitation," she said, handing the note to Mrs. O'Flaherty. "It is from Lady Jane Dibbley, wife of the governor."

"I see," Mrs. O'Flaherty said with a smile. "Dinner, tomorrow evening, at the governor's residence. I suppose I can make it."

Vi laughed. "I suppose we all can. The children will be so excited. I'm excited! Do you know anything about the governor and his lady?"

"A little," Mrs. O'Flaherty said. "Although I put my own heritage behind me when I left my home and married my dear Ian so many years ago, I never completely gave up my interest in the British aristocracy. Lady Jane is a

Montcrieve—an ancient and noble family. Her title is hereditary, so she is addressed as 'Lady Jane' rather than 'Lady Dibbley.' Her great-grandfather—or perhaps great-great-grandfather—was the royal governor here in the last century, and he amassed a large fortune in the sugar trade. Lady Jane is, I believe, of an age somewhere between you and me, in her early forties. She had an older brother, but as I recall, he died fighting in the Crimea. I do not think that she has children. Unless there are some cousins I never heard of, Lady Jane is the last of the Montcrieve line."

"Do you know anything about Governor Dibbley?" Vi asked.

"Only that the governor, Sir George, is a self-made man," Mrs. O'Flaherty replied. "The English nobility has changed much in this century. Men once earned their titles and their lands through service to the king or queen—fighting the wars, supplying the soldiers and money for wars, or serving the royals in politics or diplomacy. Today, it is men of industry and business—many of them commoners by birth—who receive the laurels and the knighthoods for service to the economy of the realm."

"I don't like that term," Vi said. " 'Commoners'."

"That is because you are an American, raised in a nation that declared at its founding that all men are created equal," Mrs. O'Flaherty replied. "A grand principle, though not always honored in practice."

"No, it is not," Vi sighed. "I doubt we shall ever wash away the stain of slavery."

"In Great Britain, most people are not bothered by being commoners," Mrs. O'Flaherty continued. "Perhaps that is because most people are commoners. It is not regarded as an insult but as a way of describing those who are not of the nobility. Many of England's most uncommon and extraordinary people are commoners by birth. There are, of course, some who crave titles, just as there are those who crave wealth. That is as true in the United States as in other nations."

"But we don't have noble titles," Vi observed.

"No, and that's one of many, many reasons why I am proud to be an American citizen now," Mrs. O'Flaherty said.

"Though men may separate people by wealth and social position, we are all equal in the eyes of the Lord," said Vi.

"It will be interesting to meet Sir George and see how he handles the responsibility of ruling this island," Mrs. O'Flaherty commented. "For the time being, I shall assume that he is noble by nature though a commoner by birth. I will keep some words from Isaiah 32 in mind, that 'the noble man makes noble plans, and by noble deeds he stands.' Now, should we go and rouse the children? It has cooled off a bit, and I'm ready for that walk on the square."

"I'm glad Zoe made us pack our party dresses," Vi said to her old friend as they went upstairs to the children's room. "We may be commoners, but we shall be nobly clad for our evening with Sir George and Lady Jane."

The young Raymonds were, indeed, very excited about the invitation. Had there not been so much else to see in Georgetown, the prospect of dining at the governor's house might have preoccupied their imaginations.

After their rest—and even Max had fallen asleep, despite his conviction that naps were just for babies—the children, Vi, and Mrs. O'Flaherty strolled the square and explored the small shops: a dry goods store, a stationery shop that also sold books and newspapers, a pharmacy, a furniture dealer, a bootmaker, two dressmakers and a milliner, a tearoom, and a restaurant. The street carts had disappeared, and one of the shopkeepers explained that the vendors normally came only in the mornings and sold their fruits, vegetables, and fresh fish until about noon each day, except Sunday. The newcomers also learned that the stores stayed open several hours later than stores did in India Bay. "No one except tourists wants to be out in the hottest part of the day," the shopkeeper said, "and the tourists learn our ways soon enough. We close at sunset."

At the pharmacy, Vi left a prescription for quinine that Dr. Bowman had provided, and she bought the children fruit drinks. Then they went on to see the church at the far end of the square. It was not a large building nor was it elaborately decorated, but its square steeple, topped with a plain wooden cross, made it the tallest building in the town. The first thing the children noticed was that the path to the front of the church was made not of pebbles or bricks but of broken shells which crunched loudly under their feet. On one side of the path was a grassy burial ground with a number of tombstones. The stones were clearly old, and some were broken. Lulu and Max walked respectfully among them, looking for names and dates.

Gracie did not like the look of the graveyard, so she stayed with Vi and Mrs. O. They approached the front door and climbed the few steps up to a small wooden porch. Vi was about to put her hand on the door when it swung open. Vi jumped back, and Gracie made a little squeaking sound.

A white-haired, gentle-faced man came bustling out, but he stopped instantly on seeing Gracie's surprised face. "Did I frighten you, child?" he asked with concern. "I am so sorry. I was not expecting visitors."

Looking at the ladies, he said, "How do you do? I am Reverend Smythe, vicar of this parish. Welcome to our house of worship."

Vi introduced herself, Mrs. O'Flaherty, and Gracie; then she explained that they had arrived in Georgetown that day and were staying at the Empire Hotel.

"If I may be so bold as to ask," the vicar said in his charming English accent, "what brings you to our island? Will you be with us for long?"

"For four months," Vi said, and she told him the purpose of their visit.

As he listened, the vicar smiled sweetly. "Perhaps you will join us for services during your stay?" he said questioningly.

"We would like that very much," Vi replied. "You have a lovely church, Reverend Smythe. It must have an interesting history."

"Oh, very interesting," the minister replied enthusiastically. "There was once a Spanish mission church on this site, but it was destroyed in a pirate raid on the town some two hundred and more years ago."

"Pirates!" exclaimed Max. He and Lulu had abandoned their exploration of the graveyard and came to hear what the elderly gentleman was saying.

"Yes, indeed, my boy," Reverend Smythe replied. "Georgetown has a most fascinating pirate history. Are you perhaps interested in the stories of the sea raiders who once ruled the waves of the Caribbean?"

"Yes, sir," Max said, "very interested."

"I am too," Lulu said.

Gracie didn't say anything, for she didn't think that pirates were the least bit interesting.

The vicar beamed and said, "Then you young people must come and have tea with me and my sister someday soon. I can tell you what I know of this island's pirate past, if you like."

"That is very kind of you, sir," Max said graciously. "We would enjoy that."

"I wish we could talk now, but I have several calls to make before evening vespers," the vicar said. "And I will be away from town tomorrow. What do you say to tea on Friday, the day after tomorrow? All of you," he added, looking to Vi and Mrs. O'Flaherty. "My little house is behind the church, just along the path from here."

"We would be delighted to come," said Vi.

"Good," he said happily. "I beg pardon, but I must leave now. The church is always open, so please have a look inside for yourselves. Our sanctuary is quite simple, but also rather charming, I think." Hurrying down the wooden steps, he bade them farewell and rushed along the path. "Friday at four o'clock," he called back as he left the churchyard and proceeded across the square.

Watching his rapid progress, Mrs. O'Flaherty chuckled softly and said, "The vicar is quite spry for a man of his age. I look forward to visiting with him, for I have a feeling he will have some rollicking tales to tell us."

"Well, our arrival here certainly seems a propitious beginning," Vi declared. "In less than half a day, we have already received two kind invitations and found a church to attend."

"What does pro-*fish*-us mean, Mamma?" Gracie asked. "Is it a good thing?"

"Oh, yes," Vi laughed. "*Propitious* means favorable, a sign of good things to come. Now, shall we have our look inside the church?"

4

On the Beach and Over Dinner

The sea is his, for he made it,
and his hands formed
the dry land.

PSALM 95:5

*T*he next day was passed with more sightseeing for Vi, the children, and Mrs. O'Flaherty. The hotel manager hired a carriage with a reliable driver to take them on a tour through Georgetown, followed by a picnic at the beach. The children wanted to wear their bathing costumes beneath their clothing, but Vi convinced them that they would swelter in the heat. So they packed their swimming suits and several towels in a valise. The hotel chef prepared a picnic hamper for them, and off they went.

The carriage driver's name was Henry Featherstone, and he seemed to know every inch of Georgetown. His route took them first through the quiet residential area they'd seen the day before, and he informed them that this was where "the European ladies and gentlemen" lived. He pointed out elegant town houses that belonged to some of the wealthy planters on the island, the senior diplomatic representatives of several foreign nations, including the United States consul in whose house Dr. Hockingham was staying, and one of the high-ranking English military officers. The handsome dwellings quickly gave way to much less costly houses in the same colorful style as the buildings they'd seen at the wharf. As the carriage drove on toward the countryside, the nature of the local housing changed again. Instead of neat stucco structures, they began to see small shacks made of wood and mud, with roofs of thatch or rusty tin and tattered curtains instead of doors.

Behind one shack, Vi saw several women laboring over large, steaming pots set in fire pits. Freshly washed sheets and clothing hung from clotheslines and flapped in the constant breeze that blew in from the ocean. A group of small children were playing hide-and-seek in and around the wet laundry, and several older girls sat under a low-growing tree and tended to a crawling baby. The island youngsters stopped what they were doing to wave and shout greetings at the people in the passing carriage, and the Raymond children eagerly waved back.

Leaving the outskirts of the town, they found themselves on a flat, cultivated plain, and the openness of the plain made them more aware of the large mountain that loomed in the distance. Max had brought along his compass, and he showed his sisters how the needle pointed toward the north, directly at the mountain. Henry indicated cane fields and told them that sugar was the island's main export. Vi spotted corn growing in one field.

"The first people here grew corn," Henry said. "They called it *maize*. When the Europeans came, they brought other plants, like sugar cane."

"Where did the first islanders come from?" Max inquired.

"Most people think they came up from South America in their boats and spread out over the islands," Henry replied. "Nobody knows for certain, because it must have happened a long, long time ago."

Mrs. O'Flaherty asked, "Do any descendents of the original people live here now?"

"No, ma'am," Henry said, shaking his head. "I've heard there's a few on some of the islands south of here, but all the natives—the people you call West Indians—on Christiana were killed or worked to death, or they died of sicknesses soon after the Spanish landed here back in 1500. I've heard it said that it only took fifty years for all the first islanders to disappear. Most islanders today are a mix of African and European. There's some who claim descent from the first people, and that may be true, but there's no records to prove it. It's a right shame when you think about it."

"It's terrible!" Lulu exclaimed. "All those people — just gone! How could that happen?"

"Well, miss, the Spaniards and the other Europeans who discovered the islands came for gold and riches," Henry said. "They were conquerors, and they mostly didn't care much about making friends with the natives. The ones they didn't kill, they made into slaves. But it was disease that probably did the worst of it. The Europeans and the slaves they sent over from Africa brought diseases that the original people had never had before. Something that might be just a little bother to you, miss, like a case of chicken pox, could wipe away whole villages of people who never had chicken pox before. Like you say, miss, it must have been a terrible thing — people falling sick and not knowing what was happening to them and no one much to help them."

"Did the Spaniards get sick too?" Max asked.

"That they did, from illnesses like the Yellow Jack and malaria that are common in tropical places. There was a dreadful amount of dying among the peoples from Europe too," Henry said. "But the Europeans just kept coming here and then to Mexico and down to Peru, searching for gold and silver. It's a funny thing, but the people who survived the best were the slaves from Africa, like my ancestors. Maybe that's because they came from places that aren't so different from the islands and they had some kind of resistance to the malaria and such. But that's just what I think."

"It makes good sense to me," Max said. "People from tropical climates in Africa would have a better chance of survival, wouldn't they?"

At this point Gracie leaned forward in her seat and asked, "Where did you come from, Mr. Henry?"

"Why, I come from Christiana, little miss. I was born in Georgetown and went to a school run by the nuns. For a while, I worked for the governor—the governor before Governor Dibbley, that is. But I quit, and now I have my own cab and a good business showing nice folks like you around the island."

"Why did you leave your job with the governor?" Lulu asked.

Henry remained silent for several seconds, and Vi said gently, "That's a personal question, Lulu dearest."

Lulu lowered her head, but Henry laughed and said, "I don't mind the children's questions, Mrs. Raymond. Let's just say I didn't enjoy indoor work half as much as I like being outside in the sunshine and meeting new people. Driving my cab and being a guide is a healthy way to make my living and support my wife and children. I have four children—all a little older than you but still growing up under my wing."

His answer satisfied Lulu, but Vi sensed that Henry might be evading something. She glanced at Mrs. O'Flaherty and saw a curious expression on her friend's face. *So you sensed it too, Mrs. O*, Vi thought. But both Vi and Mrs. O'Flaherty forgot their puzzlement a moment later when Henry called out, "Look over there now!"

All eyes turned in the direction he was pointing to, and they realized that the road through the fields had brought them to a place high above the ocean. They were on the top of a rocky cliff, about twenty feet above a sandy beach that spread out below like a white carpet on a sparkling blue floor. The road narrowed, and Henry's horse began to descend slowly and cautiously.

It was Max who first noticed a pile of rocks and stones that looked different from the natural face of the cliff. He stared at the formation and then asked, "Mr. Henry, is that some kind of fortification — over there — to our right?"

"You've got good eyes, young sir," Henry replied. "That's what's left of an old Spanish fort that once protected the harbor of Georgetown, back before it was Georgetown. Not much left of it now, but we can stop and take a look after you've had your swim and your lunch — if that suits the ladies."

"I think that would be fine," Vi said, "so long as we can be back at the hotel by four o'clock."

"We're having dinner with the governor and his wife tonight," Gracie declared with more than a hint of pride.

"Is that so, little miss?" was all that Henry said in reply. Then he turned his attention to the horse and silently guided the carriage down the path to the beach and onto a thin strip of grass and tropical plants that was partly shaded in the shadow of the rocky cliff.

Near the cliff, Max and Lulu found some large boulders that provided privacy as they each changed into their bathing costumes. Then they raced across the sand and into the surf, kicking the warm water and splashing each other until they were both thoroughly soaked. Mrs. O'Flaherty hoisted her parasol and went down to the water's edge to oversee their play, while Vi helped Gracie change into her bathing suit.

Gracie was not as sure of the safety of the water as were her brother and sister, and she held tightly to her mother's hand as they approached the sea. But once they got onto the wet sand and Gracie dug her toes in, she felt braver, and she laughed merrily as the incoming surf washed over her feet. She stomped about in the shallow water for a while, making it fly up around her legs in little sprays that twinkled in the sunlight.

"I like this ocean!" she exclaimed. "I like this sand!"

"It's different from the lake at Ion, isn't it?" Vi said.

"This water isn't cold at all," Gracie observed. "And it's so clear. Look at me, Mamma," she said, venturing out a few more steps into the surf and plopping herself down so that the water, though only an inch or two deep, lapped about her.

Vi could not resist. She slipped off her shoes, rolled down her stockings, and tossed them aside. Holding her skirts up above her ankles, she walked to where Gracie was sitting. Raising a hand to shield her eyes against the sun's glare, Vi looked across the glittering water. Lulu and Max were some yards farther out, both sitting on the sandy ocean floor. Yet even there, the water only came up to their waists. They were examining something Vi couldn't see.

"What have you found?" Vi called to them.

"A big shell, Mamma!" Max called back.

The two older children scrambled up and ran back to show their prize to their mother and sister. Mrs. O'Flaherty joined them and suggested a walk along the beach to hunt for more shells. Vi said that she would unpack the picnic in the meantime. So Mrs. O'Flaherty and the children headed

down the beach, and Vi returned to the carriage, where
Henry was strapping a canvas bag over his horse's head. As
Vi walked up, she heard a familiar sound—the rhythmic
crunching and munching of the horse as he consumed his
midday meal of ground corn.

Henry had already removed the picnic basket from the
carriage. Vi saw that he had also snipped some large fronds
from a low palm and laid them out on the beach to make a
kind of tablecloth.

"You don't want sand in your lunch," Henry said pleasantly.

"Thank you. That's a perfect setting for our picnic," Vi
responded with gratitude. "Does your horse need water?"
she asked, watching the placid animal eat.

"He does, ma'am," Henry smiled. "And I came prepared." Opening a trunk attached to the back of the carriage, he lifted out a heavy tin container with a fitted lid.
"Can't count on finding fresh water except during the rainy
season, so I brought my own. There's another bucket in the
boot, in case you folks have need. But I know the hotel provided your drinks."

"Where do you get fresh water when it isn't raining?" Vi
asked curiously.

"From the mountain, ma'am. The weather's different up
there, and it rains nearly every evening, all year round. If
you watch the mountain near sunset, you can see the clouds
forming up high. The storms up there send water down the
streams to irrigate the fields, feed the wells in the countryside, and collect in the town reservoir. It's very good water,
Mrs. Raymond. I know that newcomers are afraid of the
water, and that's smart of them in most places. But we've
got good water in Christiana, thanks to the old governor,"

Henry said. Then he told Vi how the previous governor had hired French engineers to build the reservoir and a water and drainage system for Georgetown. "The old governor — Sir Percy Wilberthorne — had an idea that clean water would make for less disease. He also put the soldiers at the garrison to work draining the swamps on this side of the island. I didn't know his reasoning, but Sir Percy was something of a scientist. Whatever his thinking, we haven't had any big outbreaks of fevers since the water system was finished. We were all very sorry when Sir Percy got called back to London. I hear he's over in India now."

"Does the new governor keep up Sir Percy's enterprises?" Vi asked.

"Well, the water and drain pipes are still working, but I don't see any new work being done," Henry replied. "The new governor spends money on other things."

"When did Sir Percy leave Christiana?"

"Three, almost four years ago, ma'am. Maybe we'll get a new —"

Henry broke off just as the horse shook his head and whinnied. Though the animal did not seem to be complaining, Henry quickly undid the strap on the feedbag and removed it from the animal's head. Ladling some water from the bucket into a shallow wooden bowl, he held the bowl to the horse's mouth, and the horse lapped noisily.

"Just a little now," Henry said softly. "And a little more before we go back to town. You can have your fill when your day's labor is done."

The breeze blowing off the ocean carried the sound of children's voices. Hearing this advance warning of her family's return, Vi hurried to unpack the picnic basket. "Please join us for our meal," she said to Henry, as she set out plates

and cups. "We would all enjoy hearing more about the island while we eat."

The driver turned to her with surprise in his face. "No," he said after a moment. "No, but thank you, ma'am. I brought my own food."

"Then sit with us while you eat," Vi persisted. "You have made our lovely table," she added with a smile that brought out her dimple, "and we would be honored to have you join us."

"Well…" Henry began, drawing out the word as he made a decision. "That's very kind of you, Mrs. Raymond. I'll be pleased to sit with you."

The children had collected many shells on the beach, and Mrs. O'Flaherty's pockets were filled with their finds. She dumped the shells out, and the children sorted them by size as they ate their lunch. Henry told them about the different types of shells and the sea animals that had lived in them, and he also warned them against picking up shells that still contained living animals. "Mostly, they're harmless," he said, "but a few got poisonous bites that can make you sick. It's best not to gather shells out of the water, just to be safe. The shells are like the old fort on the top of the hill. The animals live inside, and the shells protect them from bigger, stronger creatures. If you stick your finger into the shell or put one up to your ear, the little living thing inside will think it's under attack. You'll get so you can tell the difference between empty shells and the ones that are still home for one of God's creatures."

The picnic meal was quickly eaten, for the children were very hungry after their play in the surf and their walk. Vi checked her watch and said, "If you hurry and dress, we have just enough time to see the old fort before we go back to the hotel."

As the children ran off to get their clothing, Henry helped the ladies gather up the remains of the picnic. He was putting the horse's feedbag and the bucket of water into the carriage trunk when Vi said to him, "We will be on the island for four months, and we are in need of a guide. Would you be available to help us, Mr. Featherstone?"

Henry smiled and said, "I'd be glad to be a guide for you and your family, Mrs. Raymond. If you like, I can suggest some tours that might interest the children. You tell the hotel manager whenever you need me. He knows how to find me."

"That's excellent," Vi said happily. "I think you are a historian, Mr. Featherstone, and a keen student of the natural world. We can learn much from you. I want us all to learn as much as we can during our visit here."

"It's my pleasure to tell you what I know, ma'am," he said. "I'll do my best for you."

Mrs. O'Flaherty had just finished getting Gracie dressed, and they approached the carriage as Vi and Henry were talking. A few moments later, Lulu and Max ran up and got into the carriage, helping Gracie in after them.

Looking around to see that nothing had been left behind, Mrs. O'Flaherty glanced at Vi and chuckled. "Vi girl," she said, "I believe you have forgotten something."

Puzzled, Vi said, "What, Mrs. O? I've gathered up all the picnic belongings, and the children are all here."

In amusement, Mrs. O'Flaherty lowered her eyes, and Vi followed her friend's gaze until she finally realized what was amiss. Her own feet were as bare as the day she was born.

"My shoes and stockings!" Vi exclaimed. "I left them on the beach!"

Scurrying across the sand, she found her footwear and stockings just where she'd tossed them. Returning to the carriage, she raised her shoes and turned them over, letting loose a considerable rain of sand, accompanied by the laughter of her three children.

After they saw the old fort, Henry returned them to the hotel at a few minutes before four o'clock. This gave everyone plenty of time for a bath and a rest before dressing for their special dinner, and they were all ready when Mark got to the hotel. He had to rush to dress, so the children didn't have a chance to tell him about their picnic and their new friend Henry Featherstone. But Mark promised to give the children his undivided attention before bedtime, for he was very interested in hearing about their first day on the island. His own first day had been long and tiring, as he, Dr. Hockingham, and their team members organized their supplies and tools and packed the carts they would take on the expedition.

Mark went to his bath, while Vi laid out his clothes in their room. He felt much better after he had washed away the dirt and dust. And he was very glad to have a few minutes alone with his wife as he quickly donned his evening attire.

"I fear I won't be good company tonight," he said, as Vi helped him buckle his vest and then re-tied his evening tie, which Mark had made a mess of in his hurry.

"You're always good company," Vi said.

"Hah!" Mark snorted. "You better than anyone know that I am *not* always good company, especially when my mind is on my work. But I shall do my best, my dear, for I do not want to offend the governor or his lady by falling asleep at their dinner table."

"Did you have a very hard day?" Vi asked solicitously.

"Not really," he said, as she patted his now perfect silk tie. "I have to adjust to the heat and the humidity. That's all," he explained. "It's a necessary phase in the tropics. The physical labor is good for me."

"It must be even harder for Dr. Hockingham," Vi said, "at his age."

Mark laughed easily and said, "Hockingham is not much given to physical labor, my dear. His forte is giving directions. Yet he is as strong as a horse, even at his age, so do not concern yourself for his health. He's a wonderful fellow, Vi, a remarkable scholar, and the best of companions, but he is not a laborer. We all have our roles to play, and Hockingham's role does not include lifting and toting. When we see him tonight, he will not show the slightest sign of fatigue."

"Yet you don't resent his — ah — his lethargy?" Vi wondered aloud.

"Not in the least, for it isn't sloth. His other abilities far outweigh his physical limitations. In the search for antiquities, Hockingham has the nose of a bloodhound. If there is anything to be found on this expedition, he will point us to it," Mark replied.

He slipped on his jacket, tucked a handkerchief into his pocket, and gave his thick hair a last, quick brush. Then he took Vi's arm and said, "I'm as ready as I will ever be to meet the governor. And you, my darling, look dazzling. If I feel the least bit sleepy, I need only glance at you to be restored."

"You are a dreadful flatterer," Vi said, playfully poking his arm.

"You disapprove?" he said with a look of mock surprise.

"Oh, no," Vi laughed. "I enjoy *your* flattery."

"Then let's be on our way, me beauty," he said in a rakish way.

"You sound like a swashbuckling corsair," Vi laughed as they left the room.

"A poor corsair," Mark replied with a grin, "for I have no ship to sail upon the briny blue. By the way, how are we getting to this party?" Mark asked.

"A carriage is being sent for us," Vi said. "I imagine it is waiting for us now."

The governor's residence was located just outside Georgetown, not far from the English military garrison. Despite its proximity to the town and the garrison, the house seemed isolated, set back from the main road and shielded from view by lush tropical plantings and undergrowth. The driveway was dirt but changed to gravel when they reached a wide, open space and the house came into view. The carriage driver told his passengers that it had been built in the 1830s and was one of the largest houses on the island. The long, low structure seemed to rest on a platform several feet off the ground, and its red tiled roof protruded beyond the house itself and over a wide porch that extended across the front and around the sides of the structure. The exterior was of white-painted wood and stucco. Dormered windows set in the sloping roof indicated that the house had two stories. It was surrounded by a well-tended garden that included a sweeping front lawn. To Vi's artistic eye, the house and grounds were pleasing in their simplicity.

Violet's Foreign Intrigue

Two men—one black and one white—were standing on the porch, obviously awaiting the guests' arrival. The white man came forward to greet everyone, while the black man assisted Vi, Mrs. O'Flaherty, and the children from the carriage. The white man—tall, extremely thin, and too young to be Governor Dibbley—spoke with a British accent that indicated he was not an islander.

Smiling in a strange, tight way, as if he were not accustomed to using his facial muscles for such an expression, the young man bowed slightly and said, "Welcome, Professor Raymond and Mrs. Raymond. I am Robert Wigham, personal secretary to his lordship, Governor Dibbley. The governor extends his apologies. He is in a meeting and will be available very shortly. Lady Jane is in the parlor. If you will follow me now…"

He gestured toward the house and proceeded up the wide wooden steps. The family followed. Lulu tugged at Max's sleeve and whispered, "Do you remember Mr. Eric, with the Melanzana Circus?"

Max nodded, and then he smiled at his sister, for he knew what she meant. Mr. Wigham, the governor's secretary, looked very much like Mr. Eric, the thin and dour circus "giant" whom they had gotten to know during their first summer in India Bay.

"I wonder if Mr. Wigham has a tiger like Mr. Eric?" Max whispered to Lulu. He was about to say something else, but catching a sharp glance from his father, Max fell silent.

They were led into a wide hall with polished wood floors and a series of heavy doors on each side of the passage. At the far end of the hall was a curving staircase, and the back wall of the hall was made entirely of glass doors that framed the green landscape beyond. A number of large, old-fashioned portraits in gilt frames hung on the pale gold walls, and crystal chandeliers were suspended from the ceiling.

Mr. Wigham went to the second door on the right, knocked, and entered. "Your guests have arrived, Lady Jane," he said, motioning to the family.

A small, elegant, and very pretty woman was rising from her chair as Vi and Mark went in. Lady Jane came forward and extended her hand to the couple. Then Mark introduced Mrs. O'Flaherty and the children. Lady Jane seemed genuinely pleased to have them as her guests and gave special attention to each of the children. Inviting them to be seated, she resumed her own place in a high-backed, brocaded chair.

The conversation began easily as Lady Jane asked questions and listened closely to the responses. She inquired about the Raymonds' lodging, their activities since their arrival in Georgetown, and their first impressions of the island. To Mark, she said, "I am very interested in learning about your expedition, Professor Raymond, but perhaps we should wait until Dr. Hockingham arrives to have that discussion."

"A good idea, your ladyship, for my colleague takes great pleasure in explaining our work," Mark replied. "I would not want to steal his thunder, because he is not only informative but also very engaging."

"You and Dr. Hockingham are partners in this venture?" Lady Jane asked.

"Technically, I am the leader, for my university is funding the expedition," Mark explained. "But in every way, I regard Dr. Hockingham as my partner."

"That's good," said Lady Jane with a gentle, almost wistful smile. "Very good. The best results are usually attained by true partnerships."

A young native woman entered with a tray of cool drinks. She was wearing a white dress and starched white apron, and her hair was completely hidden under a brightly patterned headscarf in yellow, green, and blue. The colors of her scarf and her dark bronze complexion made her aquamarine eyes, large and fringed with thick black lashes, all the more brilliant. It was only when the young servant lowered her eyelids that Vi realized how lovely her face and how graceful her stature were.

The maid passed the drinks without comment and quickly left the room. For some reason, Vi was sorry to see the girl go and hoped to meet her again, in less formal circumstances.

A few minutes later, Dr. Hockingham was shown into the parlor. With him was a man whom Vi knew a great deal about but had not met in person. It was Malachi Bottoms, the artist who had been a member of Mark's archaeological expedition to Yucatan a year and a half earlier. Vi had often studied his drawings and watercolors from that trip, and she'd wondered about the man himself. As another round of introductions was made, Vi observed the artist, who was, much to her surprise, not much older than herself. Of medium height and build, he had black hair, worn longer than was the style and somewhat shaggy at his collar. His brown eyes were smallish but bright beneath thick and unruly eyebrows. His nose was longer than most and finely shaped, and his lips were thin, though his smile was generous and perhaps, Vi thought, a little mischievous. Vi also noticed that although Mr. Bottoms was correctly attired, he did not seem altogether comfortable in his suit, starched shirt, and tie.

The two new arrivals were seated, and the maid returned to serve them drinks. The conversation went forward, and Vi noted how adept Lady Jane was at seeing that everyone was included, even Malachi Bottoms, who seemed inclined to shyness.

Another quarter of an hour passed before Governor Dibbley came to join them. At his entrance, it was as if the whole room were electrified by a burst of energy. His mere presence was so strong that even before he said a word, he was the focus of attention. The governor was a tall, handsome, well-built man of about forty-five years. He was deeply tanned, and his dark brown hair was streaked with blonde that spoke of much time spent in the sun. His eyes, beneath wiry black eyebrows, were a golden shade of hazel, and his black mustache curled upward at the ends, emphasizing his prominent cheekbones and giving him a slightly roguish look.

Everyone, save his wife, stood at his appearance, but the governor waved his hand and said, "Thank you, but let us not be formal this evening. We are in the tropics, not our good Queen Victoria's palace. Ladies, please resume your seats." Striding confidently across the room, he went to the eldest member of the party and said, "Dr. Hockingham, I presume."

"Indeed, sir, I am," Dr. Hockingham replied with a gleeful smile and an awkward little bow. Then he introduced the rest of the guests, and Sir George greeted each one graciously. Once he had taken his chair, he turned to Mrs. O'Flaherty and said, "It is a special pleasure to meet you, madam. On Lady Jane's and my last visit to London, we attended a symphony concert at which the music of your late husband was featured. A pastoral. It was brilliant. I believe that you assisted with the orchestration. Am I correct?"

Mrs. O'Flaherty was used to receiving such comments on her husband's musical works, but she was surprised that Sir George knew of her contribution. "I did work on the original orchestrations, several years ago, with Maestro Vivante, who introduced my husband's work to the world. But how did you know of my participation?"

"I have a good memory for names," the governor said with a warm smile. "The pastoral by Mr. Ian O'Flaherty so touched me that I studied the concert program carefully and noted your name. Then I inquired of a musician friend, and from him, I learned the story of your determination to have your husband's genius recognized. It is not a story easily forgotten. As I recall, my friend said that you are also a musician."

"Not of my husband's rank, of course," Mrs. O replied, "but I do play and sing."

"Then perhaps you will entertain us at some time," the governor suggested. "We in the islands often feel starved for music performed with excellence."

"I would be happy to," Mrs. O'Flaherty agreed.

Sitting back in his chair, Sir George turned to Vi and said, "I hear that you, Mrs. Raymond, and Mrs. O'Flaherty run a Christian mission in your native South. What a noble undertaking. Tell me of the services you offer there."

It was Vi's turn to be surprised at the governor's knowledge, for she could not imagine how he might have heard about Samaritan House. She told him briefly about the mission, and he asked several intelligent questions. He mentioned Reverend Smythe, the local Anglican vicar, who was trying to organize similar services on the island. The governor seemed very pleased to hear that Vi and Mrs. O'Flaherty had already met the vicar and were to see him for tea the next day.

"Fine fellow," the governor said of the reverend. "A bit unrealistic at times, but I suppose that's in the nature of his calling. Still, he preaches a good sermon, and he's very good company over dinner. Yes, indeed, our vicar is a fine churchman. You will enjoy knowing him."

Vi wanted to ask what Sir George meant when he said the vicar was "unrealistic," but the black man who had greeted them entered the room and announced that dinner was ready. The governor rose and gave his arm to Mrs. O'Flaherty. Mark escorted Lady Jane; Vi took Dr. Hockingham's arm; and Mr. Bottoms, smiling shyly, offered to escort Lulu and Gracie (which pleased both girls enormously). Max followed them into the dining room, where a long table, draped in white, was set with beautiful china and silver and graceful arrangements of native flowers. Two men in white jackets helped the ladies be seated, and the men and Max filled out the table. Vi and Mrs. O had instructed the children about the etiquette of dining, so the children kept their eyes on Lady Jane. The servants placed bowls of soup at each place, but only when Lady Jane took her first spoonful of the clear, delicious-smelling liquid did the young Raymonds dare to raise their own spoons and begin the meal.

Sir George started the conversation by asking Mark and Dr. Hockingham about their expedition. Dr. Hockingham told him about the site they had selected at the north of the island. When the governor inquired why that particular area was of interest, Mark explained, "Our theory is that the Maya of Yucatan may have crossed to the islands by boat. If that is so and if they made landfall on Christiana, the northern site seems the most likely place. Dr. Hockingham and I have studied the earliest maps of the island, as well as sea charts and the writings of the early European explorers, for clues."

"But how did you come to your theory in the first place?" Sir George inquired.

"We found some items — carved stones — during our dig in Yucatan two years ago," Mark responded. "The ancient writing of the Maya is, as you may know, inscrutable to us, though I believe it will be accurately translated. The best source now is images — paintings, carvings, and the like. The carved stones we found include a symbol for what we believe is a boat unlike those that would be used by fishermen. It may be only a symbol, of course, but our hypothesis is that it may represent a ship capable of crossing deep waters."

"And you have mounted your expedition on the basis of a single symbol?" Sir George said, unable to hide his incredulity. "No maps? No written descriptions of such a voyage? Just a single symbol?"

With a chuckle, Dr. Hockingham interjected, "The older the history, the fewer the clues, Sir George."

"It is an interesting theory," the governor conceded. "The area you are going to explore was once frequented by privateers and pirates, for it is secluded and sparsely populated. It was a good place for pirates to hide and divide their spoils between raids on the Spanish fleet."

"You are interested in pirate history?" Mark asked.

"It is something I have been reading about lately," the governor said. "I am not a student of the subject, but it was a time of adventure and daring that has a romantic appeal for me. I am quite content with our present level of civilization, however, and more than happy that the skull and crossbones no longer fly on the ships of the Caribbean."

Both Lulu's and Max's ears had pricked up at the mention of pirates and their infamous skull and crossbones flags, but when the governor left the subject to inquire more about the archaeological expedition, the young Raymonds went back to their food, which was exceedingly good. After dessert, Lady Jane invited the ladies and the children to return to the parlor with her, while the men took their coffee at the dining table. The evening wound down most pleasantly, and on the ride back to the hotel, Vi, Mark, and Mrs. O'Flaherty spoke highly of Sir George, Lady Jane, and their hospitality. With a yawn, Max said that he thought the governor would make a fine pirate, but that was the only comment heard from the Raymond children. In the open carriage, beneath the clear and starry sky, first Gracie, then Lulu, and finally Max fell soundly asleep—a fitting reward after such an exciting day.

CHAPTER

5

Lady Jane's Second Invitation

As you enter the home,
give it your greeting.

MATTHEW 10:12

$\mathcal{V}$i let the children sleep late the next morning, and she and Mark enjoyed a walk around the town square before their breakfast. They both wanted to make the most of their time together, and they cherished these infrequent periods alone. Their discussion was mainly of practical concerns, but what meant most to them was the closeness—walking arm-in-arm, sharing glances, and making little jokes between themselves.

"I shall miss you, my darling Professor Raymond," Vi said as they turned back toward the hotel. "When do you think you will be able to return from the site for a visit with your family?"

"In a month," he said, taking her hand and pressing it quickly to his cheek. "Hockingham's two students will be arriving to join the expedition, and I'll come to town to get them and replenish our supplies. I wish it could be sooner, Vi. I wish I could go off to the site each morning, as I go to the university in India Bay, and return to you each evening. I have grown pleasantly accustomed to my life as an ordinary family man and husband."

"But I would not have you be an ordinary man," Vi replied with a dimpled smile. "I married an adventurer, and while I shall miss you more than I can say, I would not have you any other way."

"Nor would I change our lives by a hair," he said. He was silent for several moments as they walked on. They were just passing a tall hibiscus tree when he stopped suddenly, pulled his wife into his arms, and kissed her firmly upon her soft mouth. It was a spontaneous moment, and neither Mark nor Vi realized that they were in full view of the cart vendors and early shoppers in the square. A few of the shoppers observed the couple and smiled at this display of loving affection.

An elderly woman buying fruit pointed a finger at the Raymonds and asked the fruit vendor, "Are they English?"

"No," the vendor answered with a chuckle. "The lady and her children bought mangoes from me yesterday, so I know. She and her husband are visitors from the United States."

"Ah, that explains everything," the shopper said. She lifted a melon from the cart and sniffed it for freshness.

"What do you mean, missus?" the vendor asked.

"Americans are often impetuous, I think," the woman said. "They do not always hide their feelings so easily."

"You are not shocked, missus?" asked the vendor, with a twinkle in his eye.

"How could I be shocked by an expression of true and righteous love between husband and wife?" the old woman responded huffily. "Remember your Bible, man, for it tells us that love comes from God. It is clear that the lady and her husband are much in love. Now, how much will you charge me for this ripe melon?"

Unaware of the little stir their kiss had caused in the marketplace, Vi and Mark proceeded to the hotel, holding hands and whispering like newlyweds.

Mark left the hotel after breakfast with the family. He and Dr. Hockingham planned to finish all their preparations no later than the middle of the next day, which was

Lady Jane's Second Invitation

Saturday. They wanted the local members of the expedition team to have time with their families and to share a worshipful Sabbath before they all set out from Georgetown on Monday morning.

The hotel manager had recommended a sightseeing trip for Vi and the children to a nearby sugar plantation, and Vi had arranged for Henry Featherstone to be their guide. There was no need for a picnic basket this time, for the tour would include a luncheon at a restaurant that specialized in native dishes.

Having slept longer than usual, the children had dressed hurriedly, gobbled their breakfasts, despite Mrs. O'Flaherty's warning that they would all have indigestion, and were waiting on the hotel's front porch when Henry's carriage arrived. They climbed into their seats and said good-bye to Mrs. O, who had decided to remain at the hotel and write letters. Vi was just walking out the front door when the young boy who was apparently the hotel's chief messenger ran up to her and handed her a white envelope. She instantly saw that it was exactly the same as the envelope she'd received from Lady Jane Dibbley two days earlier. Hearing Gracie call to her, Vi handed the boy a coin, tucked the letter in her skirt pocket, and quickened her steps. Although curious about what Lady Jane might have written, Vi decided she would read the note later.

The tour of the plantation proved both interesting and educational for the young Raymonds, none of whom had thought much about the source of the sweet white crystals that made Miss Moran's cakes and cookies so delicious. They learned about the growing of cane and how it was changed into raw sugar and then shipped to the major ports of Europe and North America, where it was refined. They saw how the cane was harvested by workers using large blades called *machetes* and then crushed to extract the sweet juice and how the juice was boiled to remove the moisture and leave the raw sugar crystals.

Henry Featherstone explained the process so clearly that the children never lost interest. Vi's impression that Henry was a historian was confirmed when he told them how sugar and molasses played a role in the American Revolution. "The British wanted to stop smugglers from selling Caribbean sugar and molasses to the American colonists," he said, "so they put a high tax on sugar from the French and Dutch islands here in the Caribbean. The American colonists didn't like that the least bit, and they raised a ruckus until the tax was lowered. That was in 1764, and it wasn't too long before your ancestors were protesting just about everything the British did. By 1776, the Americans were so tired of British rule that they were ready to fight for their independence."

"Are smugglers the same as pirates?" Lulu asked.

"Not quite the same," Henry said, "but similar."

It was just past noon when they left the plantation. The restaurant was not far away — a good thing since the children were very hungry after their morning's activity. Unlike the restaurants they were accustomed to in India Bay, this one was a simple, whitewashed house with bright blue shutters at the windows. It was not large but had a wide stone veranda that provided a view of the ocean. There were tables and chairs in what once was a parlor, where several guests were already enjoying their midday repast. The hostess, a woman about Vi's age, with lively brown eyes and light brown curls peeking out from her head scarf, greeted them cheerfully. Speaking English with a pleasing French accent, she suggested that the family might enjoy having their lunch on the veranda, and when Vi agreed, she led them out to a table beneath a wooden bower covered with dark green vines.

"*Tres bien*," the hostess said as the children and Vi seated themselves. "Would you like a menu or perhaps you would prefer our *specialite du jour*? Today we have a lovely fresh fish in sauce, served with rice and vegetables from our garden and a *salade* of fruits."

"We understood that you served native cuisine," Vi said wonderingly.

The young woman smiled and said, "Ah, but we do, madam—island cuisine with a touch of France. I think you and your *enfants* will find it a delicious combination."

When Vi and the children agreed that they would all have the special fish, the young woman smiled again, brilliantly. "Ah, *tres bon*," she said. "And I shall serve you in the style of the family."

The children were trying to decide what "the style of the family" was when the woman returned with a large bowl filed with thick slices of crusty bread, a crock of bright yellow butter, and plates and knives for each of them. "Take what you like, and I will see that the bowl is kept full," she said as she left them. A few minutes later, she was back with large glasses of fresh juice, and she promised that the fish would be ready soon.

The young Raymonds each took a piece of bread and then went to explore the veranda and its views. Left alone, Vi remembered the envelope in her pocket. Searching her purse, she found her eyeglasses; then she opened the letter. She expected only a courtesy note following on the previous night's visit to the governor's house; she had posted her own note of thanks to Lady Jane during her morning walk with Mark. But reading just a few lines, she saw that it was another invitation—and quite extraordinary.

After some kind words of pleasure at meeting Vi, Mark, and their children, Lady Jane had written:

> The Empire is a very nice hotel, but it is not home, and I fear that it will surely become confining for you after a week or so. I think, and my husband agrees, that you, your children, and Mrs. O'Flaherty might be more comfortable staying here with us. We have a guest house not far from the main house, which offers four bedrooms and all the conveniences. There is also a staffed kitchen, although I hope you will share meals with us as often as possible, and the children would have full use of the grounds for play.
>
> If you have no other plans, please join me for tea on Sunday afternoon, and I shall show you the guest house. Once you see it, you can decide whether it is suitable for your needs.

The note was signed "Lady Jane Dibbley." But there was also a second page, written in the same hand but more hurriedly, as if Lady Jane had dashed off her postscript at the last moment:

> You would be doing me a great kindness to stay here, Mrs. Raymond. I rarely have the company of other women anymore, nor of such beautiful children. You will all be safe and well looked after, I assure you. Come at three o'clock, and you shall see.

Vi had just read the note a second time when the young French woman appeared bearing two large bowls. Behind her was an older man swathed in a white apron and holding out a large platter that seemed to be heaped with leaves.

"*Allo, allo!*" the man called out, and Max, Lulu, and Gracie came running to the table. The man set down the platter, and with a theatrical flourish, he lifted away the leaves to reveal a large, flatish fish complete with head and tail.

"*Le poisson grand en feuilles!*" the man exclaimed with a big grin of pride. "*Pour la famille Americaine! Bon appetite, madam. Bon appetite, mes enfants!*"

The three young Raymonds stared at the fish — Max and Lulu with curiosity and Gracie with an expression of something between shock and fear. Her little face had gone pale except for two bright spots of red on her cheeks.

"Did he say 'poison'?" Gracie gasped.

"Oh, no, dearest," Vi said, taking her youngest onto her lap. "He said *poisson*, which is the French word for 'fish'. He said 'the big fish in leaves for the American family.' And it is a magnificent fish, fresh from the sea and cooked inside what I believe are banana leaves."

"You are correct, madam," the young Frenchwoman said. "It is a native method that keeps the fish very tender and moist. It is my papa's specialty."

"Looks very *bon* to me," Max said as he watched the man expertly cut into the fish and lift the succulent flesh from the bone.

"But it's looking at me!" Gracie exclaimed. "Its eyes are looking right at me! Miss Moran never cooked us fish with the head still on."

"Well, we won't eat the head or the tail," Vi told her. "Just the good part in between. That's what *bon* means —

good. I imagine the head and tail will be used to make broth for other tasty dishes."

"That is just what we will do, madam," said the woman. She placed a plate of fish, colorful vegetables, and aromatic rice before each of the Raymonds. Seeing that Gracie's color had returned, Vi slipped the little girl off her lap and helped her into her chair. Gracie picked up her fork but hesitated. She looked at her sister and brother, who were already eating with gusto. She glanced at her mother as Vi lifted a piece of fish to her mouth. Only when Gracie was thus reassured did she taste a very small piece of the *poisson*.

"It's okay," she said a little grudgingly. Then she ate a larger piece.

"Try the sauce," Lulu said. "You can taste coconut in it. Yum!"

Satisfied that the family was well taken care of, the French chef and his daughter went to other duties. The meal was delicious, Vi thought, and the setting was splendid. She would have to remember to thank the hotel manager for his excellent recommendation. She was sorry that Mr. Featherstone had not accepted her invitation to dine with them this time, but he had brought his own food and preferred to share his lunch hour with his horse.

They were just finishing when Lulu said in a worried tone, "Oh, Mamma, we forgot to say grace. We forgot to thank our Heavenly Father for this wonderful meal."

"You're right, Lulu," Vi replied in surprise. "But we can tell God now how grateful we are for His bounty and thank Him not only for our food but also for our enjoyment of it. Perhaps you would say our prayer for us."

They all clasped hands and bowed their heads. Lulu began, "Thank You, Lord, for this meal. We're a little late telling You, but we really are thankful for such good food and such a nice place. Dear Lord, please bless this restaurant and the people who made our lunch for us and Mr. Henry who brought us here. Oh, and thank You again for letting us come to Christiana. Amen."

The family got back to the hotel in plenty of time for Gracie to have a short nap before their afternoon appointment with the vicar. Lulu and Max took their books and went down to the hotel lobby to read, and Vi and Mrs. O'Flaherty relaxed on the hotel's garden terrace.

"Did you finish your letters?" Vi asked her dear friend.

"Every one of them," Mrs. O replied with satisfaction. "I wrote to your mother and to Dr. Bowman and Emily. I also wrote to several friends in New York and to an old acquaintance in London."

"How productive you've been," Vi said. "I have written to Mamma as well as Miss Moran and Kaki and our friends at Samaritan House, but I haven't been nearly as prolific as you. I am impressed."

"I am not always so attentive to my letter-writing, but I found myself wanting to share my impressions of this beautiful place and its hospitable people with my friends," Mrs. O'Flaherty replied.

"I have something to share with you," Vi said, taking Lady Jane's letter from her pocket and handing it to her friend. "I want your opinion."

Mrs. O'Flaherty read the note quickly. "Well," she began, "I think it is a jolly fine offer, if the governor's guest house suits us. What do the children think?"

"I haven't told them yet," Vi said. "I didn't want to get their hopes up until I discussed it with you and Mark. He has mentioned the possibility of our renting a house here in

Georgetown. Like Lady Jane, he worries that the hotel is not entirely suitable for all four months of our stay."

"Yes, it may become confining after a while," Mrs. O mused, "especially for Max and Lulu and Gracie. They need safe places to run and play, and I can imagine few places as safe as the governor's compound. It also sounds to me as if Lady Jane would genuinely welcome our company." With a wide grin, she added, "Assuming that the house meets everyone's approval, I say that we should accept her invitation."

When Mark came in to change his work clothes for attire appropriate for tea with the vicar, Vi showed him the note. He was very enthusiastic. "I think you should accept if the house meets your approval," he told his wife. "From a purely selfish perspective, my darling, it would ease my mind to know that you and the children are under the protection of the governor while I'm away. Not that I think there is any danger to you in Georgetown—far from it. But if there were an emergency, if one of the children became ill, for instance, all the governor's resources would be right there for you."

"I've thought of that too," Vi agreed with a smile. "In fact, I cannot come up with a single negative that would prevent us from accepting." She quickly kissed his cheek and said, "While you finish dressing, I'll write Lady Jane and tell her that we will be happy to join her for tea on Sunday afternoon. I do have a good feeling about this, Mark. I think it will be a memorable experience for all of us."

Lady Jane's Second Invitation

Reverend Smythe's small house was almost completely hidden behind the church and further sheltered by a small, tidy garden. The house, which the vicar shared with his widowed sister, Mrs. Smiley, was furnished with many items that, judging by their worn and faded appearance, were of some antiquity. Every flat space seemed to be topped with china figurines, glass vases and bowls, wooden boxes, lace doilies, and other odd knickknacks whose purpose was a mystery. But the house was very inviting, in its overstuffed way.

"I brought my furniture from England when I came to the islands," the vicar explained cheerfully as he escorted the Raymonds and Mrs. O'Flaherty into the sitting room. "My sister brought her furniture when she came here after the death of her husband. So, you see, we are abundantly blessed with chairs and tables and whatnot."

He introduced the visitors to his sister, whose name was an apt description of her personality, for Mrs. Smiley smiled most sweetly most of the time. "I am at fault for the clutter," she said when everyone was seated. "I transported far too much when I came here, but I was so attached to everything after my husband, the late Mr. Smiley, passed away. Each thing seemed filled with good memories of him and our thirty-one years together. Now, of course, I know my folly. The Lord keeps Mr. Smiley's memory alive in my heart—not in my furniture." Then she smiled at the children and said, "Now tell us all about yourselves, my dears."

The afternoon passed pleasantly in the company of the gentle vicar and his kind sister. Mr. Smythe informed them about the history of the Christiana Islands, and remembering his promise to the children, he told them several stories about pirates who once used Christiana as their base of operations. But he changed the subject when Mrs. O'Flaherty happened to mention Samaritan House. The vicar suddenly wanted to know everything about the mission and its work, and the Raymonds and Mrs. O were happy to indulge his interest.

When their guests were leaving, Mr. Smythe and Mrs. Smiley invited them to Sunday service at the church and also to come to tea again on Sunday afternoon. Mark said that the family would certainly be at church but that they had a previously scheduled appointment on Sunday afternoon.

"Perhaps some other day then," Mr. Smythe said. "I want to hear more about your mission in India Bay."

Smiling broadly, his sister said, "My brother delivers an excellent sermon, as you shall hear on Sunday, but his chief dedication is to the people of the island. He has often talked of a mission or a clinic, and I believe he plans to pick your brains on the subject."

On the short walk back to the hotel, Lulu asked her father, "What appointment do we have on Sunday afternoon, Papa? You told Mr. Smythe that we have 'a previously scheduled appointment.' I thought we were going to spend Sunday with you, before you go on the expedition."

Mark tugged playfully at Lulu's long braid and said, "You have very sharp ears, my girl. Indeed, I had planned to spend the day entirely with you, but something has come up that will take us back to the governor's house for a couple of hours on Sunday."

The children began to barrage their father with questions that came so fast Mark could not get a word out. Laughing, he held up his hands and exclaimed, "Whoa! Slow down! Now, that's better. Vi, will you tell these curious rascals about the invitation from Lady Jane? Give them all the details, for they shall be as much a part of the decision as you and Mrs. O'Flaherty and I."

Vi quickly told them about Lady Jane's proposal and how they would tour the governor's guest house on Sunday. "We will make our decision after we see the house. It might not be suitable for us, you know, so don't get too excited yet."

Vi's final caution, however, evaporated on the breeze. In the imaginations of her three children, they were already packing for their next move.

6

The Expedition Begins

Whatever wisdom may be,
it is far off and most
profound — who
can discover it?

ECCLESIASTES 7:24

ecause Reverend Smythe was a vicar of the Church of England, the service he conducted was unfamiliar to the young Raymonds and also quite interesting, so they paid close attention. His sermon, based on Matthew 19:13-15, seemed almost to be written for them, for Mr. Smythe spoke eloquently of the love of Jesus for children and the responsibility of adults to love and care for all children by raising them in the love of the Lord. Even Gracie, who was still inclined to fidget during sermons she did not understand, was caught up in the reverend's words and barely moved a muscle.

"I really liked what Reverend Smythe said," Gracie whispered to Lulu as they were leaving the church. "It made me think about Mamma and Samaritan House and how good everyone there is to all the children. It made me think about Polly, and how I don't have to worry about her because she's at the mission and it's a house of love."

Lulu gently squeezed her little sister's hand and replied, "I liked his sermon too, because it made me think. It's not just adults who should love children like Jesus did. We children have to love and be kind to each other."

After lunch, Mark asked the children to help him finish his packing, and then everyone prepared for their second visit to the governor's residence. Once again, a carriage was sent for them, but this time, Lady Jane herself was waiting on the porch for their arrival. Sir George was away. He often traveled to outlying parts of the islands and might be gone for several days, she explained.

"Before we have tea, I thought you might want to tour the guest house," she said. "It is one of my favorite places, and I hope you will like it."

They had not seen the guest house on their first visit because it was located in a forested area behind the rear garden. It was not a long walk from the main house, yet it seemed to materialize magically amidst the sheltering trees and bushes. The single-story structure, constructed of unpainted wood and native stone, was low and close to the ground, so it blended into the landscape until one was almost upon it.

"This is the house where I was born," Lady Jane said as she mounted the front steps and opened the door. "My father brought my mother here when they were first married."

"You grew up here, Lady Jane?" Lulu asked in surprise.

"I did, my dear, and very happily. I am a native of the islands," Lady Jane said, and they all heard the happiness in her tone as she spoke of her childhood. Suddenly, she didn't seem at all like the gracious and sophisticated wife of the royal governor, but more like a perfectly ordinary friend as she continued. "My grandfather built the big house and this house, which my father inherited and then passed on to me. The family compound was part of a large sugar plantation then, and my grandfather named it Gilead, for the Bible tells us that Gilead was rich in healing spices and medicines. I will tell you the whole story sometime, but now, let's look around."

The guest house was not at all like the elegant main house, except in its spaciousness. Its design was plain, and the central rooms seemed to run together, creating a large, open space. Light flowed in from many tall windows. Where most houses had walls, this one had great timbers supporting the ceiling. The tiled floors were covered with large mats of woven grass. Most of the furniture was rustic and appeared very comfortable, but a few pieces—the dining table and chairs and a large sideboard among them—were of European origin. Vi was struck by how well this mixture of native carpentry and English antiques went together. The kitchen, Lady Jane said, had once been a storage room but it had been re-done and was quite modern, except for its wood-fired stove and ovens. To the back of the house were four bedrooms, all with real walls and wide windows, and two bathing rooms.

"If you girls don't mind sharing," Lady Jane said to Lulu and Gracie, "there should be plenty of space and privacy for everyone." The girls were more than willing to share, and Max was more than glad that he would have a room to himself.

Guiding her guests back to the central rooms, Lady Jane ushered them through a glass side door onto a wooden porch built several feet above the ground. The land around the sides and rear of the house had been cleared of vegetation and the twenty feet or so between the house and the forest were covered with the same kind of white shells that the Raymonds had first seen on the church path. The cleared space allowed the sunshine to enter from above and light the house.

"I understand why this is your favorite place, Lady Jane," said Mrs. O'Flaherty. "It is like an enchanted cottage in a fairy tale."

Smiling beautifully, Lady Jane asked, "Do you think it will meet your needs? I do hope so, for it would give me such pleasure to have you stay here."

Mark looked at his children, who were beaming, then at Mrs. O'Flaherty, and finally at Vi. "I can tell from your faces," he said, "that you are ready to move in. Lady Jane,

I feel confident in saying 'yes,' and I'm sincerely grateful for your generosity."

"That is splendid," Lady Jane replied with a sigh of relief. "It is really you who are being generous. I think we should go to the main house and have our tea. We can discuss plans for your move, though I promise not to keep you long. I know that the professor leaves tomorrow, and you will want this evening together."

Over tea in Lady Jane's sitting room, it was decided that the move would be made in two days. As the time for the family to go approached, Lady Jane told Vi that she would send the governor's carriage to the hotel and a cart for their luggage. Vi said that wasn't necessary, as the family had an excellent local driver and that Mr. Featherstone would be glad to bring them.

Lady Jane's expression clouded slightly. "Featherstone? Is that Henry Featherstone?" she asked. When Vi said it was, Lady Jane lowered her voice and said, "Henry should not come here. You see, Henry was employed as a bookkeeper for the previous governor—a high post for an islander—and he continued in that job for Sir George. Then Henry and my husband had some kind of disagreement, and—well—it was uncomfortable for all of us. I do not want to put anyone in a difficult situation now."

Lady Jane paused, and Vi thought she saw mist in the woman's eyes. Then Lady Jane said in the gentlest way, "How is Henry? It has been a long time since I last saw him. I hope he and his family are doing well."

"Very well," Vi replied. "May I tell him that you asked?"

"Please, do," Lady Jane said, touching Vi's hand briefly. "Henry is a fine man and a godly man. I am still unsure about the cause of his break with my husband. I am certain it was just a misunderstanding, but it would be best if he not come here." She paused again before adding, "Tell Mr. Featherstone that I said I am sorry."

Vi was greatly perplexed by this, for the subject of Henry Featherstone was clearly painful to her ladyship. But not wanting to pry, Vi simply assured Lady Jane that her message would be conveyed.

"Thank you, my dear," Lady Jane said softly. Then she looked at the others and was glad to see that they had not been privy to her words. The professor and his children were studying a model ship displayed on one of the bookshelves, and Mrs. O'Flaherty had wandered to the window for another look at the view.

Vi declared that it was time for them to leave, and Lady Jane accompanied them downstairs and to the waiting carriage. All signs of her earlier emotion had vanished, as if she had locked her feelings away. But Vi believed that something troubled the lady. *Perhaps, if we become friends, I may be able to help in some way*, Vi thought. *Or perhaps just being a friend will be enough.*

The expedition team had planned to meet just after daybreak at the storage building they had rented near the wharfs. Their two large carts were already packed, and their three horses and three mules were stabled at a nearby hostelry. There were seven men in the team: Mark and Dr. Hockingham, Malachi Bottoms, Thomas Barr, Abraham Mercer, Liberty O'Dwyer, and Lorenzo Hastings. Lorenzo had been hired primarily as cook, but Mark had learned that the man also had skills as healer, which could come in handy.

Violet's Foreign Intrigue

Mrs. O'Flaherty had bid Mark farewell on Sunday evening, but the children and Vi had insisted on going with him to the storage site. Except when they had a late evening for a special occasion, Max and Lulu were early risers, so it was not difficult for them to get up at the crack of dawn. Gracie, however, was not so easy to rouse, and Vi was tempted to let her little sleepyhead stay in. Knowing, however, that Gracie would regret not saying good-bye to her father, Vi persisted and got the child dressed if not entirely awake.

Henry Featherstone had been engaged to take the family to the team's meeting place, and he was waiting for them at the hotel entrance. Mark carried Gracie to the carriage, and Max carried Mark's travel kit. Gracie finally seemed to come awake just as they reached the storage building. All but one of the men were there, checking the tarpaulins and ropes that secured the supplies, hitching the mules to the carts, and saddling the horses. Each man had a backpack, but as long as they could ride, they carried only water canteens. The sun was up, and the heat would rise rapidly as they went inland, away from the sea breeze. The less weight they had to bear, the easier the journey would be.

The children were so interested in watching the men's activity that they forgot to feel sad. It intrigued and excited them to see what their father really did on an expedition and to observe his leadership. Mark had no need to give orders because the others instinctively respected him and responded to his requests. Vi, who was also getting her first close look at her husband in his role as working archaeologist, experienced a surge of pride in his easy command and at how well the team worked together under his guidance. *They trust him*, she thought, *and he trusts them. They will keep*

each other safe. Closing her eyes for a few moments, she prayed, *Dear Lord, please guard them all on their journey and bless their mission.*

"I'm here!" a voice cried out behind her, and she turned to see a man running toward the group. A lumpy bag bounced in his arms.

"We wouldn't leave without you, Lorenzo," Mark laughed. "What do you have there? Don't tell me we have forgotten something."

Panting a little, Lorenzo greeted his leader and said, "Vegetables and fruits, Professor. We can pick our own when we get near the mountain. These are for tonight's supper."

Mark took the bag and hoisted it onto the floor of the smaller cart, on which Dr. Hockingham was already perched. The older man waved to the cook and said, "Climb up here with me, Lorenzo. You steer, and I'll navigate."

The men were all mounting to their places—Malachi and Thomas Barr on horseback and the rest in the carts. It was time for Vi and the children to say good-bye. Mark hugged and kissed his little girls; then he took Max in a bear hug, sparing him a kiss that might embarrass the boy in such masculine company. Last to feel his arms was Vi. He embraced her tenderly and whispered in her ear, "Just a month, my darling wife. I shall see you in just a month, and the sight of you will make my heart sing."

"I'm so proud of you," Vi said. "Go with God, my love."

Mark broke the embrace and hurried to mount his horse. With a last wave at his family, he turned his face toward the mountain, and the expedition began.

Vi had put several extra handkerchiefs in her pocket in anticipation of this moment, but she realized that the children didn't need them. There were no tears, no sad expressions.

Violet's Foreign Intrigue

The children watched their father and his team head down the same road they had taken on their first visit to the ocean, and their faces glowed in the rising sun.

"I'm so proud of Papa," Lulu said.

"Me too," Gracie said.

"I'm really excited for him," Max said.

"Me too," Gracie agreed once more.

"Not many children have a father who goes on such adventures," Max said. "Someday, I want to go with him."

"I'd like to be an archaeologist just like Papa," Lulu said.

Gracie started to say something, but she only got an *mm* sound out before Lulu interrupted: "We know, Gracie—you too!"

The children were laughing when Henry helped them back into the carriage. "You aren't sorry to see your father off?" he asked.

"A little bit," Lulu replied in a thoughtful way. "But Papa's going off to do work that he loves so much, Mr. Henry. We love him, so it makes us happy that he's happy. And we know that God is watching over him while he's away."

Henry turned his gaze to Vi. "You've got three very wise young ones there, missus."

Vi only smiled in response—a beautiful dimpled smile.

When they reached the hotel, the children rushed inside to find Mrs. O'Flaherty, allowing Vi a few minutes to talk with Henry, telling him that the family was moving to the governor's compound and giving him the message from Lady Jane.

His face grew serious as she spoke, and when she finished, he said, "Lady Jane is an admirable person. You tell her that I don't need any apology from her. I'd like to say that to her myself, but the situation's not such that I can. Did her ladyship tell you about what happened?"

"Only that you and Sir George had a disagreement."

Henry did not speak, but Vi could see his jaw clench. Then his face relaxed and he said with a strange half-smile, "Then that's all that needs saying."

"May we still call on your services?" Vi asked hopefully. "There is so much for us to see on the island, and I believe you are the best guide there is. I can contact you through the hotel manager, and we will meet you here at the hotel."

"Why, yes, ma'am, you can do that," Henry said, with a real smile.

"Oh, good," Vi said with relief. "If you are free on Friday, I've heard there is an interesting grotto on a beach not far from the plantation we visited. Is it too far for a day trip?"

"You're talking about Captain Raven's Grotto," Henry said with a twinkle in his eye. "It's an easy ride, ma'am, and your children would enjoy it very much—especially that boy of yours who's so interested in pirates. I don't know that Captain Raven was ever there, but there's always been rumors about a buried treasure on the island, and some people think it's somewhere near the grotto."

Vi clapped her hands together. "The children will be thrilled, and this will help them take their minds off their father being away. Despite what they said, Mr. Featherstone, they will miss him terribly."

"I'll meet you here at the hotel on Friday, about ten o'clock," Henry said. "I'll brush up on my pirate history between now and then so I can spin some good yarns about Captain Raven and his treasure."

He started to climb up to the carriage seat but stepped back down to say, "I wouldn't mention to the governor that I'll be your guide. Best not to open old wounds."

"I won't," Vi promised.

She wasn't given to keeping secrets, but in this case, she felt that she was making the right choice. Whatever had occurred between the cab driver and the governor, something deep inside her told her that Henry was not to blame.

The transfer from the hotel went smoothly, and Vi, Mrs. O'Flaherty, and the young Raymonds were settling into the governor's guest house before noon the next day. Their new kitchen was well stocked with food, and Vi and Mrs. O were considering what to prepare for lunch when there was a knock at the door. It was Lady Jane and the young maid Vi remembered from their first visit to the Gilead compound. They were carrying baskets, and Lady Jane said, "I thought we might enjoy a picnic on the porch. I also wanted to introduce Beatrice Rowan, whom I have asked to tend to your needs during your stay."

"How thoughtful of you, Lady Jane," Vi said. "And I am very happy to meet you, Beatrice. Let me take that basket, Lady Jane."

Basket in hand, Vi went to the kitchen, with the young maid following her. Vi started to unpack the food, but Beatrice said, "I'll do that, missus. You go and chat with her ladyship while I ready your lunch. Let's see now, there's five of you and Lady Jane — six places." She quickly surveyed the kitchen and checked the ice box. To herself, she said, "Good. Rafe remembered to put in a fresh ice block."

"I hope we won't create too much bother for you, Beatrice," Vi said. "You must have other duties."

Beatrice looked at Vi with an amused expression. "No, ma'am, there's no bother at all. I'm to be your full-time attendant while you're here, so you won't be taking me away from anything. I've got a feeling that I'm going to enjoy this job."

Vi went to find her ladyship and saw her on the porch with Mrs. O'Flaherty. Joining them, Vi said, "Beatrice seems to have everything under control."

"She is a fine young woman," Lady Jane replied, "as intelligent as she is lovely. She will be leaving us soon to go to England."

"What will she do there?" Vi asked.

"Go to school," Lady Jane answered with a wistful smile. "She will live with an aunt of mine in Devonshire and attend a church school, training to be a teacher. I shall miss her greatly. But she plans to return to Christiana when she finishes her course."

"To teach here?" Mrs. O'Flaherty asked.

"That is our plan," her ladyship answered.

The ladies seated themselves, and Lady Jane told her guests a little more about Beatrice, who had grown up on the plantation. It soon became clear to Vi that Beatrice held a special place in Lady Jane's heart.

They talked of other things until Mrs. O'Flaherty excused herself, saying, "It is very quiet inside. I think I should check on the children."

This gave Vi a chance to tell Lady Jane that she had spoken to Henry Featherstone.

"Did he accept my apology?" Lady Jane asked.

"He said there was no need for one," Vi replied.

"That is what he would say," sighed Lady Jane. There was a soft look in her eyes, but she quickly recovered herself. "Bless you, Mrs. Raymond, for conveying my message. You must be curious, and I appreciate your discretion."

Vi, who was indeed very curious, flushed slightly. "I do want you to know that I have engaged Mr. Featherstone to be our guide on another sightseeing trip on the coming Friday. The children have taken a great liking to him, and he has impressed us all with his knowledge of the island history and lore. But if this will cause any…"

She paused, and Lady Jane asked if he would come to Gilead to get them. When Vi explained that they would meet him in Georgetown, she thought she caught a hint of disappointment in Lady Jane's eyes. Yet again, however, a veil was almost instantly brought down on Lady Jane's feelings.

"Then I will arrange for our butler, Rafe, to take you into town on Friday," Lady Jane said. "It's best that way. In fact, you will have a carriage and driver at your disposal as long as you are here."

"That is kind," Vi said with a smile. "I am skilled at the reins. My father taught me to drive when I was growing up on our plantation, and I can manage anything from a buggy to a hay cart. If I may have access to a buggy, then there will be no need to take one of your drivers away from his work."

"Excellent!" Lady Jane declared. "So you too grew up on a plantation—something we have in common. I will introduce you to our stableman so that you can make your travel arrangements with him whenever you like. I do not want you to feel that you must consult me about your plans. I want you to feel at home while you are here, and that includes the freedom to come and go as you please."

"Perhaps you might join us for one of our sightseeing jaunts," Vi said, hoping she was not being too forward.

"Ah," Lady Jane mused. "Perhaps I shall. Perhaps…" Her voice trailed away.

The porch door swung open, and the three young Raymonds emerged, carrying plates, tableware, and linens. Mrs. O'Flaherty followed them.

"We're helping Beatrice," Gracie happily told Vi. "She's so nice, Mamma. She's going to take care of us while we're here."

The table was quickly set, and Beatrice produced a fine meal for everyone. When Lady Jane asked the young woman to share their lunch, Beatrice said, "Thank you, ma'am, but I want to run back to the house and get some more towels for the kitchen. I told the children I would help them put their clothes away and then show them around the gardens, if that's all right with you, Mrs. Raymond."

"It is all right if you allow me to accompany you on the tour of the gardens," Vi replied.

And so the Raymonds and Mrs. O'Flaherty began their first day in the governor's guest house at Gilead. Lady Jane proved to be the most thoughtful of hostesses, seeing that all their needs were met but intruding very little on their privacy. She never went to the guest house without sending a note first, yet she encouraged the Raymonds and Mrs. O to come to the main house as often as they liked. Over the next few weeks, they would often dine with her and the governor when he was at home. They all enjoyed seeing the governor, whose charm never seemed to fade. Yet Vi began to sense that Lady Jane lived a lonely life. Although she was often busy with official duties for Sir George, her ladyship rarely left the compound, except to attend church services, and never went with her husband on his business travels. Nor did Lady Jane entertain on her own. No ladies ever called in the mornings, and Lady Jane apparently did not host the luncheons and teas and card parties that were the normal routine for the wives of high-ranking government officials and diplomats. Vi started to wonder if she and Mrs. O'Flaherty were Lady Jane's only female acquaintances.

Each time she came to the guest house to chat with Vi and Mrs. O'Flaherty, Lady Jane grew more open and lighthearted. She frequently talked about her happy childhood on the island, and she told them how hard it had been to leave Christiana when she was twelve and her family moved to England. Only one area of conversation seemed off-limits, and that was anything related to her marriage. Vi, who struggled against leaping to conclusions about other people, nevertheless found herself worrying about her new friend's happiness.

In every other way, the new living arrangements were successful. The children began their lessons on the day after they moved, and though they had enjoyed their "holiday," all three were eager to return to their studies. The Friday outing to the pirate's grotto was a treat, and Henry Featherstone came prepared with fascinating stories about the mysterious pirate, Captain William Raven, who had once made Christiana his base of operations and mounted fierce sea raids against the Spanish galleons that were filled with gold, silver, and precious gems bound for the coffers of the royal court of Spain. Henry told the children that

Captain Raven may have been a renegade English naval officer working secretly for the British Crown. But others maintained that he was Dutch or French. It was said that Captain Raven hid his treasures somewhere on the island, but no one had found them, though many had searched. When the children asked what had happened to the pirate, Henry said that no one knew. There were stories that he and his crew were all killed when the ammunitions on their ship exploded and the ship sank with all hands aboard. But there were also stories that Captain Raven had taken his treasure and gone to Africa or the Far East, where he'd lived like a prince.

Vi wished that Lady Jane could have been with them. Vi had asked her and seen a light in Lady Jane's eyes. But it had flickered out quickly. Sir George had returned and was entertaining some important military officers from the nearby garrison. It was Lady Jane's responsibility to plan the party and see that everything went perfectly.

Seeing that flicker in Lady Jane's eyes—could it have been the light of hope? Vi wanted, against her own better judgment, to find out what had happened between the governor and Henry Featherstone and why it weighed on Lady Jane. Vi prayed to her Heavenly Father for His guidance. He did not resolve her concerns about Lady Jane, but Vi knew that He had answered her prayer when these words from Psalm 31 came to her: "But I trust in you, O LORD; I say, 'You are my God.' My times are in your hands...."

Thank You, Lord. You always tell me what is right, she prayed, *and You have taught me to be patient when I am tempted to take the wrong path. I think You want me to be patient now and not to force myself rashly into a situation I don't yet understand. I*

will abide, Lord, but please help me overcome my curiosity and strengthen me against my inclination to leap before I look. If Lady Jane needs my assistance, I trust in You to tell me when the time is right. I am in Your hands, dear Lord.

7

The Mountain

*Guide me in your truth and
teach me, for you are God
my Savior, and my hope
is in you all day long.*

PSALM 25:5

The Mountain

There is only one complaint I have about the guest house," Vi said to Mrs. O'Flaherty. They were standing on the north veranda of the main house at Gilead and waiting for the call to supper with Sir George and Lady Jane.

"What complaint?" Mrs. O'Flaherty asked.

"Being so close to the ground and enclosed by the tall forest, the guest house affords us no view of the mountain," Vi said. "In this spot, however, I can look up and see the mountain rising in the distance and feel closer to Mark. I suppose that's silly, but when I look at the mountain, especially at this time of day, I know that Mark and the men are returning to their camp and that Lorenzo is preparing their evening meal. I imagine them sitting around their fire and discussing today's work. In my imagination, I can see the light slowly fading and Mark lighting his lantern, and then he and Dr. Hockingham working into the night as they plan for tomorrow."

Vi's voice softened and took on a dreamy quality as she went on, "I miss Mark most of all at this time of day, Mrs. O. If we were back in India Bay right now, he would be coming home from the university. Oh, he might be a little late, if he has been meeting with his students, but I don't worry. The children would be doing their homework by the fireplace in the living room and listening for the sound of Mark's carriage. I might be helping Miss Moran in the kitchen, or more likely, I would be in the library, doing some bookkeeping or correspondence for Samaritan House. But my concentration would be less than perfect, for I would also be listening for the carriage and Mark's footsteps."

Mrs. O'Flaherty wrapped her arm gently around Vi's waist and said, "Then your dear professor would come in the front door, and the family circle would be complete again."

"That's it, Mrs. O," Vi said. "The family circle. I did not know before this trip how the family circle completes me, and I thank God every day for bringing Mark and the children into my life. I used to think that I might never marry, that our work at Samaritan House was so important that my life was too full for anything else. Yet how much stronger I have become because of Mark and Max and Lulu and Gracie. The Lord has truly blessed me with our little family circle and with you and our friends."

Mrs. O'Flaherty smiled and said, "Circles within circles, my dear. When we love the Lord and follow His commands, we love one another, and the love we give comes back to us. I think that the best way to bring others to the knowledge of our Heavenly Father's incomparable love is to extend our own love outward. Imperfect as we are, love is the greatest gift we have to offer our fellow inhabitants of this world."

"Circles within circles," Vi responded thoughtfully. "And at the heart of every circle is the love of our Lord and Savior. God is love, and all that is good in us flows from Him."

The two women stood in silence for some time, gazing at the mountain and pondering the expanse of God's love.

They did not hear the approach of a tall, thin man, and both of them jumped when Mr. Wigham said, "Good evening, ladies. The view from here is beautiful, isn't it?"

"Yes, it is," Vi said. The secretary's remark had caught her unawares. During the last three weeks, she had grown accustomed to Mr. Wigham's presence in the governor's house, but she had not managed to feel comfortable with him. On several occasions, both she and Mrs. O'Flaherty had attempted to engage him in conversation, but nothing seemed to interest Mr. Wigham beyond his work for the governor. Even simple questions, such as where he had lived in England and how he had come to his present job, elicited the briefest replies and no real information. He was polite but always distant and, Vi believed, secretive. She did not dislike him, but after his repeated rebuffs, she was inclined to ignore him.

His comment on the beauty of the view was a surprise because it was so out of character. In light of her conversation with Mrs. O, Vi decided to make another attempt with Mr. Wigham.

"The mountain intrigues me," she said. "The way it rises from the sea, it seems so solitary and still and ancient. It makes me think of a pyramid rising from the desolate sands of Egypt, though I have never been there."

"And yet, this mountain is no remnant of ancient history, for it is capable of renewed activity at any time," Mr. Wigham said. "There are great forces underneath its quiet exterior. When it erupts again, it will alter this island, as it has done in the past."

"But it is quiet now," Mrs. O'Flaherty said, the barest hint of a question in her tone.

"Yes, ma'am, and there are no signs that it will come to life anytime soon. You may rest assured. The mountain is sleeping like a lamb," Mr. Wigham replied. Lowering his voice, he added, "But it will awake eventually and become 'like a roaring lion looking for someone to devour.'"

Vi recognized his quotation; it was from the New Testament—1 Peter. She stared intently at Mr. Wigham, but in the waning light, she could not read his expression.

"Sir George sent me to escort you ladies to the parlor," Mr. Wigham then said in his normal flat tone. "The children are not with you tonight?"

"They were tired, so Beatrice is preparing their supper and will stay with them until we return," Mrs. O'Flaherty said.

"Ah," was Mr. Wigham's only reply, and the three of them went inside in silence.

The children were sleeping soundly when Vi and Mrs. O'Flaherty got back to the guest house after dinner. Beatrice gave Vi a good report of their behavior and then excused herself.

Settling onto a couch, Mrs. O removed her shoes, sighed with comfort, and said, "Sir George was in fine form tonight. He certainly dominates the room, but he is an excellent conversationalist, so I don't suppose that I mind. Have you noticed how he also asks questions and seems to get more in answer than people intend to say? I catch myself doing that. Tonight, for example, I told him much more about my family and my upbringing in Ireland than I have shared with anyone else save you, my girl." Mrs. O'Flaherty grinned and added, "It is a failing of age, I suppose, but a mature lady such as myself can still enjoy the attention of such a sociable and interesting man."

Vi was searching for something, and she responded almost absentmindedly, "Zoe would probably say that he is a skillful diplomat, drawing people out and storing away their information for some future use."

Vi went to the dining table and rummaged among some schoolbooks left there by the children. "I've found it," she declared triumphantly as she located her Bible beneath Lulu's Latin grammar notebook. She went to the sofa, plopped down next to Mrs. O'Flaherty, opened the Bible, and rapidly turned the pages.

"Here it is," she said. "First Peter 5:8-9: 'Be self-controlled and alert. Your enemy the devil prowls around like a roaring lion looking for someone to devour. Resist him, standing firm in the faith, because you know that your brothers throughout the world are undergoing the same kind of sufferings.' I was sure that Mr. Wigham quoted from these verses."

"Do you mean the part about 'the roaring lion'? I thought the phrase was familiar, but I was too amazed by Mr. Wigham's brief spell of talkativeness to place it. I had no idea that he had ideas about anything other than meetings, schedules, and protocols," Mrs. O said with a low chuckle.

"Did you think it as odd as I did?" Vi asked.

"Indeed, I did," Mrs. O'Flaherty said, nodding her head in agreement. "I believe he said more to us tonight than he has in the entire three weeks we've been here."

"I just realized that tonight on the veranda was the only time we have even been alone with Mr. Wigham," Vi said with animation. "He is always with Sir George or doing something for Sir George. I had begun to think of him as more of a loyal dog than a person, and for that I ask forgiveness. But what kind of person is he?"

"A more sensitive one than we suspected, to judge from his words about the mountain," Mrs. O noted. "A student of the Bible, perhaps, based on his quoting it."

"Is it possible that he was saying something beyond his actual words?" Vi wondered. "He spoke of the mountain and what lies beneath it. And this quote—this reference to the devil. These verses in 1 Peter were both a warning and a promise to early Christians who were suffering the Roman persecutions. Could Mr. Wigham have been warning us about something?"

Mrs. O'Flaherty laid her hand on Vi's knee. "I think that imagination of yours is getting ahead of your common sense. It seems more likely to me that Mr. Wigham simply let his guard down for a few moments. It may never happen again, but it certainly made me feel better about him. I think now that his odd reticence may be the result of being so much in the shadow of Sir George."

"You're probably right," Vi said. Then she giggled girlishly. "My imagination seems to have shifted into high speed here in the tropics. The colors, the sounds, even the smells of Christiana have affected my mental processes and made me open to fantasies. Promise that you will keep my feet firmly on the ground in the future, Mrs. O."

"Well, I'm not without my own imaginative fantasies," Mrs. O'Flaherty said with a grin. "Why, I have several times found myself imagining life as a member of Captain Raven's crew. Do you remember the skeleton of that wrecked ship that Mr. Featherstone showed us last week? I had quite a vision of myself, manning the crow's nest and scouting the horizon for a galleon riding low in the water under the weight of the treasure it carried."

Vi laughed aloud. "Pirates again! You are as bad as Max and Lulu with their pirate stories. And you are much too good a person, Mrs. O, ever to have been a lawless buccaneer. Whatever I may think of Mr. Wigham, at least I do not imagine him as a pirate."

As the next week progressed, Vi forgot about her suspicions of Mr. Wigham. The family grew more excited each day, waiting for Mark's return. Although he had not given them a specific date, they anticipated seeing him on the coming Thursday, because they knew that the ship bringing Dr. Hockingham's assistants was supposed to arrive on Friday. In case Mark was delayed, Vi was to meet the new arrivals and arrange for them to stay at the Empire Hotel for a night or two. This was what Mark had called their "contingency plan."

When Thursday came and went without Mark appearing, Vi was disappointed but not worried. Early on Friday morning, she took the buggy and went into Georgetown by herself. She immediately sought out the manager at the Empire Hotel in order to reserve rooms for the arriving assistants. But he had news for her.

"Your husband is already here, Mrs. Raymond," the manager told her. "He arrived before daylight, with another gentleman, and took two of your old rooms—numbers 17 and 19. He's there now, ma'am, with the doctor, and he said for you to come up if you got here before I could send a message to the governor's. He said—"

Vi didn't hear the rest. She rushed to the stairs, her mind racing as fast as her feet. *The doctor? Is Mark hurt or ill?*

The door of room 17 was ajar, so Vi rapped and entered without waiting for a response. Her eyes went straight to Mark, who was standing beside the bed. He looked up and came to her, but he didn't say a word. Instead, he guided her back into the hallway. Keeping his voice down, he said, "Malachi is very ill with fever. The doctor believes that Malachi has a chance of recovery, but the journey was hard on him. The next twenty-four hours are crucial, Vi, and he will need nursing every minute. Can you stay here with me? Can Mrs. O look after the children?"

"Of course, my love," Vi said, brushing Mark's sweat-drenched hair back from his face and looking into his weary eyes. "Are you well?" she asked, touching his brow and feeling, with enormous relief, that his skin was not hot. "I can see you are exhausted. Did anyone come with you?"

"Lorenzo, God bless him, accompanied us. He cared for Malachi the whole way, giving him native medicines that the doctor says may have saved our artist's life. We brought Malachi out of the jungle by stretcher. We'd left the cart and the animals at a small village and made our camp about two miles farther up the mountain. It was all slow going, Vi, even in the cart. Malachi was having severe bouts of fever and chills and couldn't take much movement, so I had to drive slowly much of the way. It took a full day longer than—" His voice broke, and he covered his face with his hands.

Vi put her arms around him and led him to a chair at the end of the hallway.

"When did you last sleep?" she asked gently.

"Wednesday—no—it was Tuesday night," Mark said. He managed a small smile. "We had food, darling, so it was sleep and not nourishment that we lacked."

"Then sleep is what you need now," Vi said with firmness.

"I should stay with Malachi," Mark protested weakly.

"After you've slept," she said. "I'll send a message to Mrs. O'Flaherty immediately, and then I'll stay with Malachi. But first, you go to bed. Oh, where is Lorenzo?"

"I sent him to his home to rest."

"And now it is your turn, my love."

Mark was too tired to protest further, so she helped him up and into room 19. He fell upon the bed, and by the time Vi managed to get his boots off, he was asleep. Next door, she approached the bed where Malachi lay. The doctor, who was wiping Malachi's head with a damp sponge, said, "You must be Mrs. Raymond. I am Doctor Cowden. Your husband told me that you have a good deal of nursing experience."

"I'm not a nurse, but I have helped with a number of cases including fevers," Vi told him. She looked at Malachi, who appeared to be sleeping. "This is malaria and not yellow fever?"

"It is malaria. This foolish young man was apparently forgetting to take his quinine. Although it isn't foolproof, quinine is the best protection and cure. The native herbs administered to him have been helpful, but I believe we are approaching the crisis. Do you know what that means?"

"His fever will rise until it peaks," Vi said. "We must keep him as cool as possible and get him to take liquids. The fever is dehydrating him."

"Good," Dr. Cowden said. "Do you think you can manage for a few hours while I see some other patients? I have a young mother who is close to giving birth to her first child, and I must check her. Her labor has been long, and I doubt her baby will delay for another day."

"Can you wait for fifteen minutes?" Vi asked. "I must send a note to the lady who is with my children and tell her what has happened."

The doctor told her to go along and tend to what was necessary, so Vi hurried downstairs, and getting pen and paper at the hotel desk, she wrote to Mrs. O'Flaherty, explaining Malachi's situation. She asked her friend to be sure the children understood that their father was well and to pray for Malachi's recovery.

Seeing her at the desk, the manager had come from his office to offer his help. When she gave him the letter, he promised her that he would send his most reliable man to the governor's house immediately. Then Vi remembered the two assistants who would be arriving at the wharf later that morning.

"I only have one empty room on this floor, but it is large, and I will have an extra bed set up," the manager said. "I will send someone to get the young men. Do you and your husband need breakfast?"

"No," Vi replied with a grateful smile. "My husband is sleeping, and I expect it will be hours before he wakes."

"I will make certain that your end of the hallway is kept quiet," the manager assured her.

After Dr. Cowden instructed her about the medicines to administer, he left. He wished that his own nurse was available, but she was attending to the mother in labor, who was his other major concern that day. Yet there was something about the young Mrs. Raymond that allowed him to depart in full confidence of her abilities and her dedication.

Vi's note was delivered to Mrs. O'Flaherty just thirty minutes later, and she shared it with the children and Beatrice. She explained to the children that their father was well but very tired from the journey back to Georgetown. She also assured them that Mr. Bottoms's illness was not contagious and that their parents were in no danger. She and Beatrice answered the youngsters' questions truthfully and fully. Yes, malaria could be deadly. Yes, Malachi Bottoms had a good chance of surviving because he was young and physically fit. No, he would probably not be able to return to the expedition if he lived, for it would take time to recover and regain his strength. When Max, Lulu, and Gracie reached the end of their questions, they all prayed together for Malachi's survival and good health.

They had just completed their prayer—the first of many they sent heavenward that day—when Lady Jane arrived.

"I apologize for coming without notice," she said anxiously, "but Mr. Wigham told me about the urgent message from Georgetown. Is everyone all right?"

Mrs. O'Flaherty welcomed her in and quickly informed her about the contents of Vi's note.

"Poor Mr. Bottoms," Lady Jane said. "Did Mrs. Raymond say who the doctor is?"

Mrs. O'Flaherty consulted the note again and told her it was a Dr. Cowden.

"Very good," Lady Jane said. "He is just the man I would call for fevers and any other of our tropical illnesses. But you say Mrs. Raymond is nursing Mr. Bottoms. Won't that be very stressful for her?"

Max spoke up: "No, Lady Jane. Mamma knows all about nursing. There's a clinic in her mission, and Mamma often helps the doctor and the nurse there. When she was younger, before she met Papa, she worked one summer with a famous lady doctor in New York. She nurses us whenever we're sick, and she's very good at it."

Lady Jane smiled. "I am glad to hear that," she said. "I can see how proud you are of your mother."

"There's hardly anything at all that Mamma can't do," Gracie asserted.

"Gracie, don't be so boastful," Lulu chided. "But really, Lady Jane, Mamma is a very good nurse, and she'll see that Papa gets his sleep too."

"Well, is there anything *you* need?" said Lady Jane, putting her arm around Gracie, who was pouting at being corrected by her big sister.

The three children looked one to another, and finally Lulu said, "Your prayers for Mr. Bottoms. He's such a nice man, and we're all asking God to make him well again."

"Will you say a prayer with me now?" Lady Jane asked. "Jesus tells us, 'For where two or three come together in my name, there am I with them.' Together, we will strengthen each other as we ask our Lord to strengthen our friend Malachi and to help your mother and father and Dr. Cowden as they minister to him."

They went in turn, beginning with Lady Jane. The last to offer her petition to the Lord was Lulu, and she remembered to include the men who remained at the expedition site. "Please, Dear Lord, keep them well and make them all remember to take their quinine every single day."

<hr />

Dr. Cowden came back to the hotel at noon, and he sat with Vi for about an hour. Malachi seemed no better, but also no worse. The doctor said it was a lull before the next rise in Malachi's temperature, but that the period of rest was good. When the crisis came, the young artist would need all the strength his fever-racked body could summon.

Vi wiped Malachi's face, neck, arms, and chest with her moistened cloth and gave him small sips of cool water. It was harder to get him to swallow the bitter medication, but she raised him up and held his head so the medicine could trickle down his parched throat, as she had seen Emily Clayton do. By late afternoon, when Dr. Cowden returned, her own arms and back were aching, but she felt uplifted by the fact that Malachi was still sleeping.

Dr. Cowden examined his patient. "Now, we must wait," he said. "I'll stand watch while you check your husband and get some food. Barring some emergency, I have no other appointments."

"The baby?" Vi asked curiously.

"It arrived an hour ago," Dr. Cowden said with a happy smile. "A healthy boy. Mother and child are both well, and my nurse is caring for them. Now, you must care for yourself, Mrs. Raymond. That's doctor's orders."

Vi was grateful for the respite. She had looked in on Mark several times during the afternoon, and she did not think he would wake for hours yet. She was not sleepy, and she had little appetite for food, but she wanted to wash and then take a walk about the garden to soothe her muscles and refresh herself in preparation for the coming night.

Near sunset, Malachi's temperature began to climb. He woke fitfully and was so confused that Vi and Dr. Cowden had to restrain him to keep him from pitching himself off the bed. But as his fever increased, he settled into a passive semi-conscious state. Vi and the doctor bathed him continuously, and the doctor administered doses of the quinine solution. Vi opened the windows to air the room, but for the first time since she had come to the island, there was no breeze. It was as if the night itself were holding its breath as the young artist's time of greatest trial approached.

At about eleven o'clock, Mark came in. He was still wearing his dirt-stained work clothes, but he looked rested and alert. He went to where Vi sat beside the bed and put his hands on her shoulders. "Let me take over for you," he said.

Vi did not object, for she knew that she needed a break. She stood, but because she had been sitting for so long, the tingling of pins and needles shot through her legs, and she grabbed Mark's arm for support. "I'm all right," she said quickly. "Just a bit weak in the knees."

Mark was reassured when he heard her calm, steady voice. He took her place and began to apply the damp cloth to Malachi's face and neck. Vi, feeling her circulation return, left the room and went next door to wash her face and hands and arms. Sitting down on the bed, she spoke to her best and truest Friend. "Dear Lord, Malachi is in Your hands, and I know that whether he lives or dies, You love him and will do what is right for him. But if You are not ready to take him home to You, please help us help him through his pain. Strengthen his body to fight against this terrible fever. Bathe him in Your love and mercy as we bathe him with water. Fill him with the will to live, if that is Your plan, and strengthen us to help him defeat the fever. But if his time here is ended, please, Lord, welcome him into Your Kingdom, enfold him in Your arms, and bless him with Your gift of eternal peace."

She did not know what else to say, but more words were unnecessary. God knew all that was in her heart, and as she sat there, her mind cleared, and her body revived. She felt her strength and energy returning and her aches dissipating. *God is telling me not to give up hope*, she thought suddenly.

For the next hour, Malachi's temperature continued to rise by fractions of a degree, but the increase seemed slower than it had been earlier. Then it stopped and held steady. They never ceased cooling him and praying for him, and after another hour, his temperature began to creep downward until, near daybreak, it leveled off. But it was not until they heard the sounds of the hotel coming to life that Dr. Cowden was willing to say, "I believe he will survive."

"Thank God," Mark said softly. "Thank You for delivering our friend from the valley of the shadow of death."

"We must prepare for the possibility of a relapse, for that is the awful nature of malaria," said Dr. Cowden. "I will stay for another hour, but I want you, Professor, to take your wife downstairs and get her a good breakfast. Then she needs some sleep, as I do. I will send for my nurse to watch over Mr. Bottoms today. We can discuss arrangements for his care later. Even without complications, it may be weeks before he gets his strength back."

Waving Vi and Mark away, Dr. Cowden said good-naturedly, "Go on now, you two, and follow my prescription to the letter. Breakfast and then sleep."

Thinking that the Raymonds would want some privacy after their long night, the hotel manager had set a table for them on the garden terrace.

"Dr. Cowden is sending for a woman to care for Mr. Bottoms today," Mark said.

The manager looked pleased and said, "That would be Rita — Mrs. Darling. She used to be Dr. Cowden's housekeeper, but now she's his nurse. She is almost as good at healing as the doctor himself. A mite bossy, mind you, but a fine, fine nurse."

The waiter set a large plate of peeled and sliced fruits before Vi, and the manager said, "I took the liberty of selecting your breakfast menu personally. The native fruits are like a restorative tonic, I always say. Remember, you only have to tell me what you need, and you shall have it."

They thanked him for the breakfast and everything else he had done, and flushing happily, he left them.

"Do you think our compliments made him blush?" Mark asked his wife as he speared a rosy chunk of watermelon with his fork.

"Actually, I think his pleasure arises mainly from the successful outcome of our vigil," Vi said. "He is a very resourceful manager, and his help yesterday was invaluable. He's a good man, Mark."

"And an efficient one," Mark replied. "Now eat your fruit, my dearest. Don't forget Dr. Cowden's prescription — food first and then sleep."

CHAPTER

8

Vi Steps In

Serve wholeheartedly, as if you were serving the Lord, not men.

Ephesians 6:7

Vi Steps In

Mark and Vi returned to Gilead late that afternoon with the news that Malachi's crisis had passed. After a joyful reunion with the children and Mrs. O'Flaherty, the couple treated themselves to hot baths, a welcome change of clothing, and an early bedtime. They were both well rested when they rose the next morning. It was Sunday, and the whole family attended church services with the governor and his wife in Georgetown. Then Vi and Mark went to the hotel to visit with Malachi, who was fully conscious but extremely weak. When the young man seemed determined to talk about the expedition, Mrs. Darling, the nurse, put an immediate end to the visit.

Firmly escorting Vi and Mark out of the sickroom, Mrs. Darling said, "His fever went up a bit last night. Not by much, but I will take no chances. Come back tomorrow, and God willing, he will be improved."

A compactly built woman in her sixties, with piercing black eyes, Mrs. Darling had the commanding style of a military general when the welfare of her patient was at stake, and Vi and Mark knew better than to risk her wrath. They retreated to the hotel lobby, where they found Dr. Cowden talking to the hotel manager.

"Just the people I hoped to see," the doctor called out. "I need to talk with you about Mr. Bottoms and his care. Would you join me for lunch?"

The hotel dining room was nearly full, but they found an empty table in a quiet nook at the back of the room. After a waiter took their order, Dr. Cowden said, "I want to propose something to you, Professor and Mrs. Raymond.

You have assumed responsibility for Mr. Bottoms's care, and I would like your permission to take him into my house while he recuperates. I've thought this through, so please hear me out. Even when he's better, as I am confident he will be, he cannot go back to the jungle with you, Professor. They have been very good to him here at the hotel, but he will need the kind of attention they cannot provide. I could send him to the hospital at the military garrison, but between you and me, the physician and nurses there are very competent but also very rigid about their rules. I do not think it the best environment for a young man of his artistic temperament. My house has plenty of room, a good library, and a large garden. He will have the peace and quiet he needs to recover, and I can keep an eye on him and monitor his condition. Mrs. Darling has already taken a liking to the young man and tells me that she *expects* him to move into my house. Trust me, Professor and Mrs. Raymond. If you knew Mrs. Darling as I do, you would know that whatever she expects, she accomplishes."

Mark and Vi were unable to think of any arguments against the doctor's plan, so they agreed — on the sole condition that Dr. Cowden accept payment from them for his medical services, Mrs. Darling's caretaking, and Malachi's board. The doctor hesitated at first, but seeing that the couple would not relent, he accepted.

Vi and Mark left the hotel greatly relieved about Malachi's future. Taking Mark's arm, Vi said, "I think this sounds like a good arrangement."

"So do I," Mark said.

The family and Mrs. O'Flaherty dined informally with Lady Jane and Sir George that evening. After inquiring about Malachi's health, the governor wanted to hear every detail of the progress of the archaeological expedition thus far. Mark was happy to discourse on the subject, for, in fact, the work had been going extremely well. The team had discovered what they believed were the remains of a ceremonial site of some sort.

"We do not think it was built by the Maya of Yucatan," Mark said, "for it appears to be of greater antiquity. I am guessing that it was constructed by the original natives who came to the island from Central America. There are resemblances to some of the ruins explored by John Lloyd Stephens and Frederick Catherwood at Copan in Guatemala more than forty years ago. But we know little yet, for the ruins are almost entirely buried in the vegetation. Our chief preoccupation has been clearing the jungle around the site."

"No small task, that," Sir George said. "The jungle on the mountain is more dense than in any other place on Christiana, and all attempts at cultivation have failed miserably. I haven't spent much time there myself, for I prefer the seashore and the plains."

"I have become quite agile with the machete," Mark said with a smile, "although I think that the vines grow back almost as quickly as we hack them away. And the heat and humidity sap a man's energy very quickly. I learned much about pacing the work in our first week, when we cleared a path to get the small cart to the camp site."

"Do you have enough men?" Sir George asked.

"Yes, sir, for we have been able to hire some local people from the village where our animals are being kept,"

Mark said. "Mr. Bottoms will not be able to return to the site, of course, but Dr. Hockingham's two assistants have arrived, and they both have experience in similar environments. We have adequate manpower for the work, but the loss of Malachi's talents is a problem. We need an artist."

Lady Jane inquired when Mark expected to return to the jungle site.

"In three days," Mark said. "We have supplies to purchase, and I have a few chores to attend to. Principally, though, I want to be certain that Malachi is well on the way to recovery."

Mark shared the news that the young artist would be moving into Dr. Cowden's house, which won a beautiful smile from Lady Jane. "Mr. Bottoms will be well looked after," she said. "Mrs. Darling is an excellent nurse. She—"

Sir George interrupted his wife to ask, "Can you show me on a map where your excavation site is, Professor?"

Mark turned back to the governor to answer his query, but Vi's eyes lingered on Lady Jane. The interruption had been rude, and Vi thought she had seen real anger in her ladyship's face. But within moments, Lady Jane's expression was as placid as if nothing had happened.

How does she do that? Vi wondered to herself. *How does she resign herself to being treated so ungraciously by her own husband?*

Mrs. O'Flaherty excused herself and the children so that they might stroll the gardens before nightfall, and Lady Jane invited Vi to the veranda, where they could enjoy the approaching sunset.

The men adjourned to the library, and the governor sent for Mr. Wigham, who soon brought in several large topographic maps of the island. Mr. Wigham unrolled the maps and spread them on a large table. He was quietly leaving the room when Sir George told him to stay.

"I wish we had maps as detailed as these," said Mark as he bent over the table.

"You must take this one," the governor said. "It was drawn up by French engineers who worked here some time ago. They were constructing a water system, and they went over almost every inch of the mountain, recording the elevations most carefully." He pointed to a location on the western side of the mountain. "Here is where the primary water reservoir is located."

Mark studied the map closely and then placed his finger on a spot on the eastern side of the mountain. "This is approximately where our camp is. The village is on the margin between the plain and the mountain, and our camp is about two miles farther in. The ruins are about another half-mile from the camp."

"I know that village," the governor said. "It is quite remote. The people raise their own vegetables and goats. They are self-sufficient in a primitive way. How did you know to go there?"

"From our guide, Tom Barr. His mother came from the village," Mark replied. "Thanks to Tom, we were welcomed by the elders, and they told us of some ruins in the jungle. We had anticipated looking nearer the coastline."

"I didn't know that Tom was your guide," the governor remarked thoughtfully. "You are not very far from the coast."

"Yes, I see," Mark said. "There is an inlet here and a large cove. They are not shown on my map."

"The area on the eastern side of the mountain is still largely unexplored," Sir George explained. "The French concluded that the cliffs are too steep for roadways, and that cove is barricaded by offshore rock formations — useless as a port, unless Her Majesty's current government was willing to rob the treasury for reclamation and construction. I have strongly recommended against any such project, for we have more than adequate harbors now."

"I should like to see that cove, but I am more interested in the ruins," Mark said.

"Oh. I agree," the governor said. "The cove has little to offer, I'm told, except a cave of some sort. It's a treacherous climb down by land, and they say that the beach is no more than jagged rocks. Nothing there to attract either tourists or archaeologists."

Mark agreed, but the governor's words had roused his curiosity. He began to wonder if ancient boats might have reached such a cove and landed there. It was just a thought, but Mark was unable to dismiss it entirely.

Mark returned to the guest house about a half hour after Vi.

"What have you brought?" she asked, noticing that he carried a long, brown leather tube under his arm.

"A map that Sir George has lent me," he said. "Much better than the ones we have. Would you like to see it?"

"I would," Vi said, "but you have something else to do first. The children are in their beds and waiting to say their prayers with you."

Mark's face lit up. "I've missed being with them at bedtime. It is strange, Vi, how easily we take for granted the routine habits of our daily lives, like tucking the children in at night and sitting beside the fire with you when they are finally asleep. Our routines are what I have missed most this past month."

Vi smiled, and her dimple appeared. "We can honor our routine tonight, my love, though you must wait until we return to India Bay for the fireside."

While Mark was with the children, Mrs. O'Flaherty came in to tell Vi that she planned on an early night for herself. Vi asked if her friend was tired, but Mrs. O'Flaherty said that she wanted to read a book that Lady Jane had given her.

"It's the history of Gilead, written by Lady Jane's father," Mrs. O said. "I inquired of her about the history of the plantation and how it came to be the governor's residence. She gave me the book, saying it provided the best account. So, my girl, I am going to retreat to my bed under the mosquito netting and read." Kissing Vi on the forehead, she did just that.

Something else was preoccupying Vi — an idea that had come to her earlier in the day. She was deep in thought when Mark returned to the living room and reported that Lulu and Gracie were sleeping and that Max was in bed, reading a book about the life story of the famous buccaneer Henry Morgan. He sat next to his wife on the couch and put his arm around her shoulders. Vi relaxed against him, and it was some minutes before either of them spoke, though Vi's mind was awhirl.

"I have an idea," she said at last, "and I want you not to say anything until you have heard it."

"I won't," Mark promised. "I would never interrupt you. What is this idea of yours?"

"It's quite simple, my dearest," Vi began. "With Malachi off the team, you are without an artist. I am an artist, though not nearly of Malachi's caliber. Still, I have some talent, especially for drawing landscapes and architecture. If I return to the site with you, I can take Malachi's place. You need someone to record what you find as you uncover the ruins, and I am available. The children will be safe and sound with Mrs. O and Beatrice, and Lady Jane as well, for she greatly enjoys their company and they love her. You did say that we could visit the site before we leave the island. I am only suggesting that I visit it now. I would so like to be helpful to you."

Several moments passed. Then Mark asked, "May I speak now?"

"Of course," she replied with a little giggle.

"You would have to sleep in a tent," he said.

"I have done that before with no ill effects."

"The jungle is sweltering, and there are no nice bathing tubs."

"But there is rain every night to wash away the dirt."

"Your hair will be a mess."

Vi smacked him lightly on the arm and said, "My hair is always a mess, as you well know, Mark Raymond. If that's the best objection you can muster—"

He kissed her suddenly. Then he said, "Will you forgive my interrupting you this once? In truth, my dear wife, I have no serious objections. I wish I had thought of this myself. As long as the children agree, for I think they must be included in the decision, I say 'yes'."

Vi sat up and threw her arms about him. "Oh, I am so glad!" she exclaimed. "You will have to guide me, Mark. The work will be quite different from sketching the sights of India Bay and the hills and fields of Ion. I am somewhat out of practice."

"You will do the work well," Mark said, returning her embrace. "I have never known you to take on a task that you did not do well."

"I'm no genius in the kitchen," Vi said with a sparkling laugh.

"Do you realize, my dear, that we shall be pioneers? We won't be the first husband and wife archaeological team—that honor goes to Heinrich and Sophia Schliemann, who unearthed the historical ruins of Troy. But we shall be one of the first."

Vi settled back into his arms, as Mark said, "There's one more piece of groundbreaking you will achieve if you join the team."

"What's that?"

"You will have your chance at last to wear that peculiar khaki costume that Alma made for you—the one with the pants and all the pockets," he said.

After some discussion and a good look at the map Mark had gotten from the governor, the three young Raymonds agreed that their mother should join the expedition team. Max and Lulu had no qualms about the plan and were very glad that Vi would take Malachi Bottoms's place as artist. Gracie, however, was reluctant when she was told that Vi would be gone for at least three weeks. Neither Vi nor Mark attempted to persuade her, for they didn't want her to feel any pressure. Max and Lulu, on the other hand, lost no time convincing their little sister that Vi should go. Taking her aside, they made their arguments.

"Papa really needs Mamma's help," Lulu said, "and you know that Mrs. O and Beatrice will take good care of us. Besides, the three weeks will go by faster than you think, Gracie. We've got lots to do, remember. Mr. Featherstone is taking us back to Captain Raven's Grotto, and we're going to see a parade at the military garrison with Sir George and Lady Jane. We're having lunch with Reverend Smythe and Mrs. Smiley next Sunday. And that's just this week."

"Plus, Mamma might get famous for helping Papa," Max joined in. "Just think, Gracie, our Mamma's drawings will be seen by lots of important people and maybe even printed in books and the newspapers. She'll be one of the first lady archaeologists, and boy oh boy, won't we be proud of her?"

Gracie hadn't considered that possibility. "I could make a speech about her work at school next year," the little girl mused to herself, "and tell all my friends how lucky I am to have such a brave and smart mother."

"And Mr. Bottoms would feel a whole lot better because Mamma will carry on his work until he can do it himself," Lulu added.

"And it will be an adventure for Mamma," Max said. "We're all having this great adventure, but this would be special for her. It's something we can give her back for all the good things she does for us."

Gracie thought long and hard about that reason, and she began to relent.

"Are you sure she won't be in danger? Are you sure she won't get sick like Mr. Bottoms?" Gracie asked.

"Nobody can know stuff like that for sure," Max admitted, "but the Lord will be watching over her and Papa every second of every day. I think Mr. Bottoms got sick because he forgot to take his pills. Mamma won't forget."

Gracie pondered awhile longer and finally said, "I guess it's all right with me. I'm going to miss her like I miss Papa. But I guess I'd be acting like a baby if I made her stay with us."

"You're not a baby at all anymore," Max told her. "You're nearly nine years old, and telling Mamma you want her to go on the expedition is really grown up of you."

"Yeah, Gracie," Lulu said, "really, really grown up. And if you want to cry when she leaves, that's all right too. Then Max and I will get to cheer you up. We like doing that, don't we, Max?"

"We sure do."

Gracie needed one more look at the map to be convinced. She just wanted to be certain that the expedition site was not *too* far away—not like going to England or to China—or *too* close to the top of the mountain. After Mark showed her exactly where the camp was and how near it was to the road that led back to Georgetown, Gracie said that she did want her mother to go.

"Mamma can take good care of you, Papa," Gracie said.

Hugging his youngest child close, Mark said, "No one on this earth has ever taken better care of me than Mamma, and our Heavenly Father is taking care of us all, whether we are together or apart."

"That means I don't need to be afraid, doesn't it, Papa?" Gracie asked.

"It does," Mark replied, his voice raw with feeling. "God's 'perfect love drives out fear.' If you ever feel afraid while we are away, you know who to talk to."

"To Jesus," Gracie said with a bright smile. "When children talk to Jesus, He always makes us feel better."

Violet's Foreign Intrigue

With the children's unanimous approval, Vi and Mark set out for the mountain two days later. Mark had secured a horse for his wife. Lorenzo drove the cart, and the two assistants sat on top of the pile of fresh supplies. Mark's purchases included canned foods and meats, bags of beans and rice, a number of new tools, more insect netting, Vi's drawing materials bought at the stationery shop in Georgetown, her medical kit with an extra supply of quinine, and a new canvas tent and cots. Fortunately, Vi had remembered at the last minute to put her eyeglasses into her travel kit; she would need them for the kind of drawings she expected to do.

They made good time and reached the village at the foot of the mountain ahead of schedule. The village elders were very glad to learn that Malachi had survived his fever. Mark was equally happy to learn that no one else had been taken ill during his absence. When he introduced Vi to the elders, the men of the village seemed a little surprised, but they welcomed her and presented her to their wives. The villagers prepared an excellent repast for the travelers, and Vi was accorded a place of honor at the meal.

It was late on the second day of the journey when the travelers reached the campsite. The men immediately gathered around Mark, and he quickly told them everything that happened and why his wife was joining their team. Dr. Hockingham warmly welcomed his assistants, Peter Andersen and Elijah Berman, and the old scientist also shed a few tears of joy on learning that Malachi would recover fully, for he had a grandfatherly affection for the young artist. Dr. Hockingham was greatly pleased that Vi would be part of the team. The men hurried to unload the cart and set up the new tent before the evening rains began. Then Dr. Hockingham gave Vi, Mark, and the two assistants a report on the progress made in Mark's absence.

When Vi finally lay down on her cot that night, she was very tired but also very eager to begin her work. "First thing tomorrow morning, I want to study the drawings that Malachi made before he fell ill," she told Mark.

"First thing tomorrow morning, you will eat a good breakfast, for you must be well nourished for the work ahead," Mark corrected her with good humor.

"Will I be able to see the ruins tomorrow?" she asked, her voice bubbling with anticipation.

"Yes, if you will go to sleep now," he replied with a low chuckle.

"I'm not sure I can sleep," Vi said.

"You'll get used to your cot," he said. "Just don't roll over."

"It's not the cot," she said. "It is all that lies ahead, Mark. It's the knowledge that I will be part of this work."

Mark turned down the oil lamp and sat on his own cot, which creaked under his weight.

"And why shouldn't you be part of the work?" he asked.

"It's not what people expect," Vi replied softly.

Mark laughed loudly and said, "And just when, Violet Travilla Raymond, did you ever do what people expect? Did anyone expect you to start a mission in Wildwood or face down that villainous Tobias Clinch in his saloon or rescue my runaway child in the midst of a hurricane? For that matter, who expected you to marry a pompous, self-centered professor like me and change his life forever? Now go to sleep, my adorable and unpredictable wife."

Violet's Foreign Intrigue

In the darkness, Vi felt the comfort of sleep coming over her, relaxing her weary body and her restless mind, and she did not resist it. Languidly, she said, "It wasn't really a hurricane. And you were only a little pompous." Then she drifted off as rain began to tap, tap, tap against the canvas of the tent.

CHAPTER

9

Exploring the Ruins

Can plunder be taken from warriors, or captives rescued from the fierce?

ISAIAH 49:24

Exploring the Ruins

*V*i's first days in the jungle were as exciting and challenging as she had anticipated. After studying Malachi's drawings, she had a much better notion of how to approach her own work. Mark taught her the correct use of the measuring instruments, which were vastly more precise than any measuring tape or ruler. Precision was to be the hallmark of her art work. Mark emphasized the importance of precise observation and accurate recording. He also taught her that recording the position of any find within its natural surroundings was as necessary as drawing the object itself, for its placement in the earth could provide important clues to its original use. He gave Vi several botany texts to help her identify the vegetation around the ruins, and she borrowed a geology book from Dr. Hockingham so she could learn about the layers of earth and rock beneath which much of the ruins were buried.

She worried that she might be bothering Dr. Hockingham with her frequent questions, but the elder member of the team assured her that he enjoyed nothing more than teaching so bright a pupil. When he was not available, he said, she should consult Elijah Berman, who was also a trained geologist.

Vi thought she had never learned so much so quickly in her life. After her first night in camp, she had no more trouble getting to sleep, though Mark literally had to take one or another of the textbooks she was studying from her hands before she would let herself rest.

Her first visit to the ruins surprised and briefly disappointed her, for she had imagined something more dramatic than the seemingly random rocks and stones at the center of the cleared site. Seeing the bewilderment in her face, Mark smiled and said, "It is definitely not the Roman Colosseum or the Parthenon of Athens. But we believe, my dear, that those rocks were once part of a structure built perhaps eight or nine hundred years ago, before this part of the mountain was covered by a lava flow."

Interested now, Vi asked how he could make such a guess.

"It was Dr. Hockingham who spotted these stones," Mark said. "He saw that they were unlike anything else we'd seen. Different in composition from volcanic rock. When he examined them, he found signs of human labor. Some of the stones are chipped and regularly shaped, as they would be if a person were cutting stone to build a wall. If you could get a bird's-eye view, you'd see from above that the stones form a rough square."

"A square building," Vi said, and she began to see the rocks in a whole new way.

"We think so," Mark said. "It could have been something as ordinary as a storage building or a water cistern, or it could have been a monument or temple of some kind. Maybe even an astronomical observatory. The ancient peoples were students of the heavens. All that is speculation, of course. Right now, we only know that we have found a series of stones that appear to show signs of being shaped by human hands and that they seem to be laid in a systematic pattern that may indicate human planning. Your job, dearest, is to use your considerable talent and skill to measure and draw these humble stones as we begin to dig around them."

Vi made her first sketches that day, but she was not at all pleased with her drawings. The rocks looked like rocks and the ground looked like ground, but something was wrong. That night, she consulted with Dr. Hockingham and his assistants.

Peter Andersen, who had been a student of ancient art before he discovered his calling in archaeology, finally spotted the problem. "It's the perspective that is off," he said. "Not by much, but the stones that are closest to the front in your drawings appear too large and the ones behind them seem too small. They are out of scale, and that puts your drawing off."

Thanks to Mr. Andersen, Vi recognized her failure, and the next day's sketches were much better. Each day she became more accurate in her drawings and more confident of her own ability.

While she was learning to be an archaeological artist, Vi was also learning about life in the jungle and on the island. Over supper each evening, the men talked about their homes and families and also told stories about the history of Christiana. One night, Tom Barr referred to the Christiana Islands as Nuevo Toledo, and Vi asked if that was the original Spanish name.

"It was, ma'am," Tom said. "The first Europeans to land here were Spaniards, and they honored Queen Isabella by naming the islands after her home, the Spanish city of Toledo. When the English took control, they changed the names of the islands and the main town. Our young people hardly remember the old names today. They study mostly English history now."

When Vi asked the significance of "Christiana," Peter Andersen spoke up. "I know that," he said. "The British received the islands in 1713 as a trophy of war. The Queen of England at the time was Anne. The islands were named for her brother-in-law, King Christian V of Denmark. Georgetown was named to honor Queen Anne's husband, Prince George of Denmark, whom, it is said, was very handsome and a very good husband, though not much of a politician."

"That is an odd piece of history for you, a New Englander, to know," remarked Elijah Berman jokingly to his friend.

"My grandparents came to America from Denmark," Peter explained, "and my father is a history teacher. He claims that we are somehow related to Hans Christian Andersen, the great storyteller, but I don't know. Andersen is a common surname in Denmark. I learned much Danish history in my home when I was growing up, and on rare occasions, it comes in handy."

Vi knew that the Christiana Islands included a half dozen smaller islands, and she asked if these islands had names.

"No ma'am, they don't," Tom Barr said. "They are all very small and uninhabited—big rocks in the sea, you might say."

Vi and Mark always enjoyed these conversations, for the local men's knowledge of their island and the other Caribbean islands was extensive. Tom Barr told them about Spain's long rule; Abraham Mercer proved to be quite well-informed about slavery, which had at last been ended by the British in 1834; and Liberty O'Dwyer was a gushing fountain of facts and myths from the era when pirates ruled the Caribbean.

During the days, they all concentrated on much more ancient history. The painstaking work of excavating was begun, and Vi at last saw how the tools that Mark had brought from India Bay were put to use. Mark and Peter demonstrated to Tom and Abraham how to proceed with the excavation so as not to disturb the stones in any way. Meanwhile, under Dr. Hockingham's direction, Elijah and Liberty undertook the digging of a trench that would eventually surround the area of the excavation. The trench, which was wide enough for a man to sit in, would reveal the geology of the site—the layers of rock that would tell Dr. Hockingham and Elijah about what natural forces had been at work in the past. Dr. Hockingham explained to Vi that the trench would help them to approximate the date at which the stone structure—if it really was a structure—was built. "Not an actual day or year," he laughed, "but a period of time, such as what is now called the Bronze Age. Dating what we find is one of archaeology's greatest challenges, Mrs. Raymond, and we are only beginning to develop adequate methods for measuring time."

It is as if they are digging backward in time, Vi thought in astonishment as she watched the work proceed. *Layer by layer, the earth is telling its story to them, just like reading the pages of a book. Except that this book starts at the end, and as the trench gets deeper, the story will move backward to the beginning.*

It was a difficult concept for her to grasp, so she discussed it with Mark when they were alone one evening.

"Did you ever count tree rings?" he asked her.

"Yes," Vi said with a smile. Mark's question brought back memories of her childhood, when her father showed her how to count the rings in the stumps of newly felled trees at Ion. "The rings tell us how old a tree is. Papa said they can also tell us about the weather conditions in each year of the tree's life. He said that a very narrow ring indicated slow growth, perhaps as the result of a drought, and a wide ring showed rapid growth during a year when both rain and sunshine were in abundance. Papa said that by studying the rings, we could learn about patterns of weather."

"Oh, I understand!" she exclaimed suddenly. Her eyes and her smile widened, and even in the lamplight in their tent, Mark could see the sparkles in her eyes.

"The layers of rock are like the rings of the trees," she said. "Each layer speaks of what was happening to the earth at the time the layer was formed. Earthquakes, floods, ice, even fire, I imagine."

"Indeed, even fire," Mark said, enjoying his wife's excitement, "but fire on a massive scale, like the fiery lava flows that formed this island. Time has left us a record of earth's complex history in the rocks.

"The more we learn of our earth's past, Vi, the greater our awe and wonder at His creation becomes. The earth truly is full of His glory, as the Scriptures proclaim," he added.

" 'In the beginning God created the heavens and the earth,' " Vi said. "That is the first Bible quotation I ever learned, yet I think I am only beginning to understand those words. Here, in this jungle, I am seeing as if for the first time the incomprehensible vastness of God's creation and the meaning of the responsibility He has entrusted to us. 'Then God said, "Let us make man in our image, in our likeness, and let them rule over the fish of the sea and the birds of the air, over the livestock, over all the earth, and over all the creatures that move along the ground." ' I think the work you are doing—exploring the past—will help us become better stewards by increasing our awe at the wondrous earth that He has created."

"I have long thought that my work must honor Him," Mark said with intensity.

"It does, my dear husband. I see that so clearly now," Vi said, taking his hands in hers. "Your work honors past and present, which He created when He created day and night. Time was His first gift to us, and we must use it well, to glorify Him."

Mark's smile returned. "God also gave us the seventh day to rest," he said. "Tomorrow is Sunday, when we honor Him by laying down our picks and shovels and even our pencils and drawing pads. We conduct our own service on Sunday, because we have no church to attend."

"But we do have a church," Vi said, "for His creation that is surrounding us now is our house of worship."

In Vi's second week at the camp, she noticed that Mark and Dr. Hockingham were spending more time each evening poring over the map that the governor had given them. When she inquired about this new interest, Mark said that he was thinking about taking two or three days to explore an area northeast of their present location.

Laying the map out for her to see, he pointed to a large cove. "Sir George discouraged me from going there," Mark said, "but Dr. Hockingham and I both think the cove may offer more evidence to support our theory that the original island people arrived here by a sea route. According to Sir George, the cove is now barricaded by rocks and too difficult for boats to enter. But we think that the coastline was altered by the last volcanic eruption. Prior to that event, we think it may have been a hospitable harbor.

"This is a convenient time for me to be away," he continued. "We can't proceed on the ruins themselves until the trench is completed, so we are shifting all the men to that task. I will take Elijah with me."

Vi said in a teasing tone, "I am sure I can occupy myself productively for two or three days. When will you leave?"

"Will tomorrow morning suit you?" he asked.

"What suits you is what matters," she replied seriously. "I will miss you, dearest, but you must not worry about me. I really do have work to do. I can use the time to check all my measurements again, and I would like to do some water-color renderings of the ruins."

"We will be able to remove the surface stones when Elijah and I return, and then the excavating will resume. Hopefully you will soon have new subjects for your pencils to record," he said. "Your drawings really are top-notch, Vi. I can admit to you now that I worried you might not be able to adapt to so disciplined a form. What I have always loved about your art is its freedom and energy—both qualities that are not present in stones."

Vi laughed. "Stones certainly do not have energy, unless one throws them. I'm glad that I haven't let you down, Mark."

"In truth, dear wife of mine, you have lifted me and all the team up," Mark replied with a grin. "In fact, I think you should accompany me on all future expeditions. Having a woman on the team is a civilizing influence."

Mark and Elijah left just after breakfast the next morning. They wore packs on their backs, slung water canteens over their shoulders, and carried machetes to clear their path. Except for binoculars and a compass, they took no scientific tools, for the purpose of the trip was, as Mark said, "to get the lay of the land."

The next two days passed quickly for Vi. She accomplished the tasks she had set for herself and began a new project, collecting samples of the vegetation around the ruins and researching them in a botany textbook lent to her by Peter Andersen. She found some small flowering plants that were not in the book, and Peter became very excited, thinking that perhaps she had discovered a new species. At his suggestion, she made careful watercolor paintings of the plants and recorded their measurements and location with the same precision she applied to the ruins.

On the afternoon of the third day, she began watching for Mark and Elijah. When there was no sign of them by suppertime, she grew a little anxious. So after the meal, she decided to occupy her mind with reading, and she retired to her tent, but every bird call or snapping twig startled her and broke her concentration. Then the rain began. *Unless they are very close to camp, Mark and Elijah will take shelter for the night,* she told herself. *That is what they should do. They will be here in the morning.*

Dr. Hockingham came to her tent to say good night and assure her there was nothing to worry about. Vi knew he was right, but still, her prayers were all for Mark and his companion. It was quite late before she managed to sleep.

About an hour before dawn, Elijah Berman stumbled into the camp. He had no voice to cry out and no strength left to carry him forward. He collapsed just outside the tent shared by Liberty O'Dwyer and Lorenzo Hastings.

Lorenzo was always the first to rise. He would light the cooking fire and put a large pail of water on to heat before he washed himself in the small stream that cut through the undergrowth about ten yards from the camp. The sky above had turned purple-gray, and even though the forest hid the horizon, Lorenzo knew the sun was about to come up. He left the tent and took a deep breath before going to his work. He took just two steps before his foot caught on something and he fell forward. By twisting his body before he hit the ground, he managed to land in a sitting position. In the pale, gray light, he saw that his legs lay across Elijah's chest, and he heard the young man moaning. Scrambling to his knees, he put his hand to Elijah's neck and heaved a sigh of relief when he found a strong pulse.

Oddly, Lorenzo had not made any other sound since leaving the tent, not even when he fell. Now he called out full force for Tom Barr. The tall guide, wearing only his trousers, came at a run. He bent over Elijah and said, "What's happened? Where's the professor?"

"I don't know, to both questions," Lorenzo said. "I think the boy's got a broken arm. And it looks like his head's cut."

Liberty had just come out of the tent. He was holding a lamp. Seeing first his friends and then the young man sprawled on the ground, he lifted the lamp. The light revealed a gash above Elijah's left eye. Dried blood covered his face and was matted in his dark hair. Liberty let out a whooping shout of "Is he dead?"

"Hush," Tom warned. "Hold that lamp so Lorenzo can see."

Lorenzo examined the gash; then he said, "It's a clean cut, not too deep. But look at his arms, Tom. See those lines around his upper arms and wrists? They look like burns—rope burns. His left arm's broken for certain, and he's got another cut across his right hand, like he was defending himself against a knife or something. Liberty, go cut me a couple of strong, straight saplings. I need to splint his arm before we move him."

Liberty hurried off, and Lorenzo whispered to Tom, "These injuries were made by a man. Elijah's got cuts and scratches from the jungle, and he mighta broke his arm in a fall. But the gashes on his head and hand and the rope burns? They're a man's work. I bet he was attacked and tied up, and somehow he got free. I can care for the wounds, but we need to get him back to Georgetown as soon as we can. A doctor needs to set that arm if Elijah's ever gonna use it again."

"We have to find Professor Raymond," Tom said sternly. "Whoever attacked Elijah probably has the professor, unless—" He paused, not wanting to give voice to his gravest fears.

"Unless what?" demanded Vi, who had been wakened by Liberty's shout. Tom and Lorenzo had not heard her approach, and she did not at first see the unconscious body over which they were bending.

At her question, Tom jumped to his feet, and Vi got a clear view of Elijah. Her instinctive reaction was to drop to her knees and, as Lorenzo had done, to take Elijah's pulse and check his injuries.

"Where is my husband?" she asked, thinking that Mark too may have been injured. "Did he tell you what happened?"

"The professor's not here, ma'am," Tom said slowly.

Not understanding, Vi asked, "Is he in one of the tents? I must see to him."

"He's not here, Mrs. Raymond," Tom said. "Only Elijah came back."

A shock of fear passed through Vi's whole body. Her stomach heaved and for a moment, she felt as if she might be sick. Tom saw her waver, and he lifted her to her feet, holding her arms tightly in case she collapsed. But beneath his hands, he felt her muscles stiffen. When she spoke, her voice was steady.

"We must find Mark," she said. "We must search for him now."

"Yes ma'am, but first we must tend to Elijah here," Tom said softly. "His arm is broken, and his hand is badly cut. We have to get him back to Georgetown and to the doctor."

The reality of the situation was sinking in, and Vi began to gather her wits. Tom was right; they had to tend to Elijah immediately. She looked down at Elijah and saw that Lorenzo and Liberty had begun splinting the young man's arm. With a calmness that surprised even her, she said, "I'll get my medical kit. We need to clean and bind that wound on his hand."

Tom walked her to her tent, where she got the kit. "We still have the stretcher we made for Mr. Bottoms," he said. "We can take Elijah down to the village in the cart as soon as Lorenzo finishes the splint and the boy's cuts are treated."

"He's coming around!" Liberty called out, and Vi and Tom hurried back to where Elijah lay, his head elevated on a pillow. Vi kneeled beside him again and started to clean his hand with antiseptic from her kit. Elijah's eyes were open, and he winced at the sting of the medicinal solution, but he didn't cry out. As Vi was wrapping his hand with gauze, he whispered, "May I have some water?"

Lorenzo brought a cup and raised Elijah's head while Vi held the cup to his mouth. He took several long drinks. Then he said in a clearer voice, "We were coming back from the cove when some men took us by surprise. We fought, but there were too many of them. They tied us to a tree. Then they left. They were gone for hours. But that gave the professor time to get my rope loose. I don't know how he managed it, for he was bound so tightly that I had to cut at his ropes with a sharp rock I found. I was about to free him when we heard the men coming. Professor Raymond told me to run and come here for help. I—I—"

His voiced failed him, and Vi gave him another sip of water.

"Don't talk now, Elijah," she said soothingly. "Save your strength."

But he shook his head, and she took the cup away.

"I have to tell you," he said with urgency. "I got away and hid until the men came back. I was trying to think of a way to rescue the professor. I was afraid that the men would hunt for me, but they didn't seem to care that I was gone. There was a man with them, and he called Mr. Raymond 'Professor.' The man ordered the others to untie the professor and take him to the cave. We'd found a cave in the cliffs. That must be what the man meant."

Falling silent again, he drank a little more water. Then he said, "I couldn't see the man's face, but I know he was the leader. And he knew who your husband was. He didn't want to hurt the professor, Mrs. Raymond. I'm sure of that."

Gently, Vi said, "Thank you, Elijah. We will find Mark, but first we must get you back to Georgetown. I'm afraid your arm is broken."

"I thought so," he said ruefully. "I fell when I was running through the jungle and hit hard on a rock."

"Do you remember how your hand was cut?" Tom asked.

"When they attacked us, we tried to fight, but the men had knives. I must have been cut then. I know one of them swiped my head with his blade," Elijah recalled.

"You're going to be all right," Vi said, "but you must rest now. I have some medicine that will help with the pain. Really, Elijah, you must rest. I promise you that we will find Mark."

He smiled at her — a weak smile, but Vi took it as a good sign. They waited for about a quarter of an hour for the pain medicine to take effect, and then the men moved him onto the stretcher.

Dr. Hockingham and Peter had been present while Elijah told his story. When Vi finally stood and left Elijah's side, neither of the men could find the right words to say to the brave young woman who, for all they knew, might already be a widow. Vi saw the combination of compassion and bewilderment in their faces, and she was deeply touched. She was also determined to begin the search for Mark.

She spoke firmly, "I believe Elijah is right and that Mark is not in imminent danger. I have a vague idea about what might have happened, but there's no time for that now.

"Tom," she said, turning to the guide, "who is your best rider?"

"Abraham," Tom replied. "He's small, like a jockey, and he can ride like the wind on a fast horse."

"Then Abraham must go down to the village now, take the fastest of the horses, and speed to Georgetown," Vi said. "He's to go directly to Governor Dibbley's house and inform Sir George of what has taken place. I will send a note to get Abraham in without delay. Tell Abraham to speak only to the governor or Lady Jane and to be very clear that my children are not to be told of this. We need soldiers from the garrison, for we cannot take on a band of armed men by ourselves."

To Dr. Hockingham, she said, "I hope you will accompany Elijah to town. It will reassure him to have you at his side on the journey. I would also ask you to go to the governor's house and speak privately with Mrs. O'Flaherty. She will decide when and how to tell the children. It is very important she know that Mark has not, to our knowledge, been hurt thus far and that I am safe and well. Will you do that for me?"

"Of course, my dear," Dr. Hockingham said. "But shouldn't you—?"

"My place is here," Vi responded. She took his hand and held it gently. "Mrs. O'Flaherty will understand that, and she will tell you that I am not inexperienced when it comes to dealing with villains. Now, I must write that note to Sir George."

She hurried to her tent and emerged five minutes later with a folded sheet of paper, which she gave to Tom. Then, realizing that she was still wearing her robe and nightclothes, Vi dressed, donning her expedition outfit for the first time. *I never imagined I would wear this on a rescue mission*, she thought as she pulled on her high boots. She grasped her Bible and clutched it to her heart. *Lord, please watch over Mark and keep him safe until we can find him. Let me stay resolute in my hope and determination. Keep my body strong and my mind clear. And let my eyes be dry so that the first tears I shed will be the joyful tears of reunion with my beloved. Please be Mark's shield and my guide. Bless him, Dear Lord, with Your mercy. And please, Lord, bless me with the wisdom to do what is right and the courage to face whatever lies ahead. Guard our children and Mrs. O'Flaherty with Your gentle spirit.*

There was a tap at her tent curtain, and she quickly completed her prayer by asking for blessings on the men, their mission, and on Elijah. Then she went out.

Tom was waiting for her. "It's possible Abraham may reach Georgetown tonight," he said. "I told him to go straight to the governor's and to gain entry no matter what the time. We've moved Elijah to the cart. I made a bed of dried palm fronds and leaves in the cart to ease the journey for him. Lorenzo is driving, and Dr. Hockingham will tend to the young man. That potion you gave Elijah seems to work good, so maybe they can make better time than when we sent Mr. Bottoms into town. That leaves me, Liberty, and Mr. Andersen to search. And you, ma'am."

Tom didn't say so, but he would have preferred that the young Mrs. Raymond also go to Georgetown. He feared for her safety, but it was also plain to him that she would not be deterred from joining the search for the professor.

"I want Liberty to stay here," Vi said. "Someone must guard the camp and be here when the soldiers come. Liberty can tell them what happened and in which direction we have gone."

Tom agreed that this was a sensible idea.

"When can we set out?" Vi asked.

"Soon," he said. "I told Abraham to send some villagers to help us. They're good trackers, and they know the jungle much better than I do. They're also good fighters, if the need should arise."

Vi bid good-bye to Elijah and his companions, remembering to give her medical kit to Dr. Hockingham. Then she made breakfast for the small group that remained. They completed preparing their packs and filling their canteens just before three strong village men arrived. If the villagers were surprised to see the young woman in a strange outfit among the team, they didn't show it.

"I wish we had the map," Vi said to Tom as they left camp.

"Don't need it, ma'am," Tom said. "The villagers know the cove and the cave. God willing, that's where we will find the professor. If he is somewhere up on the mountain, I—well—"

He didn't finish his sentence, but Vi knew exactly what he meant.

CHAPTER 10

The Secret of the Cave

He searches the sources of the rivers and brings hidden things to light.

JOB 28:11

*V*i had not before realized how dense the jungle vegetation was, because the areas around the camp and the site of the ruins had been cut back before she arrived and she hadn't ventured more than a few yards beyond the clearings. But now, as the men hacked through the undergrowth that blocked their way and the vines that snaked along the ground and threatened every step they took, she understood even more clearly why Tom feared searching in the jungle. *A person could be lost in here forever*, she thought, and a chill ran through her.

The trees grew very tall, toward the sun, and their crowns were heavy with foliage that blocked out all but the thinnest shafts of direct light. Birds called out from the lofty canopy of leaves, and Vi heard their rustling but could not see them. A low mist, the result of the previous night's rain, obscured the jungle floor and made walking even more hazardous. Everything was green — even the mist and the earth itself seemed to be tinted in a pale, glowing green. To Vi, the jungle was beautiful and mysterious but also menacing. *How frightening it must have been for Elijah to come this way alone in the dark of night.*

They had been walking for about two hours when they came to a small clearing. One of the villagers told Vi, Tom, and Peter to rest while he and his men scouted ahead. Vi was very grateful for the chance to catch her breath. The walking hadn't tired her, but the rising heat and humidity dragged at her like a restraining hand; she would not allow her spirits to fall or her confidence to waver because of the jungle. Peter, who was very fair and blonde, had turned a bright shade of red, and his hair and clothes were soaked with sweat. Even Tom complained that he felt sluggish and his feet hurt.

"How about you, Mrs. Raymond?" he asked. "Are those boots comfortable?"

"Very," she replied. "They are an old pair and well broken in. I am glad I did not bow to fashion."

"Ma'am?" he questioned.

"The friend who designed my clothes urged me to buy new boots with high heels to complement this outfit. I am glad now I decided to bring these old, flat-heeled ones instead."

Tom gave her one of his rare smiles. He was also glad about her choice, for he could not imagine trekking through this jungle with a woman in high-heeled shoes or a long dress for that matter. He thought her strange khaki suit very sensible.

Tom told his companions to sip their water whenever their mouths were parched. "If you gulp down too much all at once, it can make you feel sick," he said. Peter, who was about to take a large swig from his canteen, reconsidered and followed Tom's advice.

The villagers returned presently, and their leader, whose name was Derrick, told them there was a stream about a quarter of a mile farther ahead. After that, the jungle cleared out, so the going would be easier.

"How long before we reach the cove?" Tom asked.

"The climb gets steeper beyond the stream," Derrick said. "We've been climbing since we left your camp, but it's been gradual. When we get to the cliffs, it's almost straight up. If we can make good time through the open part, we should be able to get up the cliff before sunset."

"Have you seen any sign of where my husband and his friend passed?" asked Vi.

Derrick hesitated for a few seconds; then in a somber tone he said, "Last night's rain washed away most of their tracks, missus, but not too far back, I spotted a big rock with some blood on it. I didn't say anything 'cause I didn't want to worry anyone. I'm sure it's the place Mr. Berman fell and broke his arm, like you told us he did." Reaching into his trouser pocket, he withdrew a bracelet made of braided leather. "I picked this up near the rock. I remember seeing Mr. Berman wearing it when I was helping clear the campsite. He told me it was a gift from his fiancée."

Derrick handed the bracelet to Vi, and she also recalled seeing the slim leather band round Elijah's arm.

"That's his bracelet all right," said Peter. "A special gift, he said. I knew he was mooning over some girl back home, but he didn't tell me he was engaged. He may have thought Dr. Hockingham wouldn't take him on the next expedition if he was getting married. The doctor is sentimental about young betrothed and married couples being separated."

Vi smiled, thinking how gladly Dr. Hockingham had welcomed her to the camp. "You keep the bracelet in your pack, Peter," she said, "so you can give it to Elijah when we return to Georgetown."

The next leg of the journey was easier because the villagers had partly cut a wide path when they were scouting. The trekkers made good time and stopped at the stream just long enough to refill their canteens. One of the villagers discovered a piece of rope near the base of a thick palm tree.

"This must be where Elijah and the professor were tied up," Tom said as he looped the rope around his waist. "We're clearly on the right course. Let's be going."

About fifteen minutes later, they emerged suddenly from the shadowy jungle into a bright clearing. Instinctively, Vi shut her eyes against the light. She felt something soft and cool against her face and realized it was the ocean breeze. She opened her eyes and blinked. They were at the edge of what appeared to be a field of tall grasses. She couldn't tell how far the field extended, but in the distance she saw the mountain. *We're close now, Mark,* she thought with a renewed surge of energy. *We will have you back soon, my love, very soon.*

Tom and Derrick agreed that the party should rest again and eat. Vi passed around some cold corn cakes and meat jerky that Liberty had put into her pack. One of the villagers had picked up some coconuts, and Derrick expertly cut open the tops of the hard nuts with his machete, so they could drink the watery contents and save the water in their canteens. One of the other men then cracked the coconuts and separated the white meat from the shell. Tom said they should suck on a piece whenever they were thirsty, and they each took a share.

"There should be another stream near the bottom of the cliffs, but you never know," Derrick said. "The streams form high on the mountain, and they can shift course or disappear overnight — like the mountain just wants to remind us that it's got a mind of its own."

When they were about to set off again, Vi took a colorful scarf from her pack. It was a gift from Beatrice, and Vi tied it firmly about her head as Beatrice had taught her to.

Derrick noticed her headdress and said, "You look like a real islander now, missus."

They had reached the cliffs in good time, but the climb up the high, craggy stone was arduous and slow. The cliffs thrust outward from the mountain itself, and Derrick told them that a narrow, natural pathway began about two-thirds of the way up. Vi struggled at some of the rougher places, but Peter, who was a skilled climber, helped her all along the way. He showed her how to place her feet to get the soundest purchase on the rocks and how to pull herself upward so she had a firm hold before she moved her feet. She slipped only once, and Peter quickly grabbed her arm and steadied her.

They reached the path, which was indeed very narrow, without mishap. Following Derrick's warning to move slowly and watch every step, they cautiously made their way toward a point where the cliff flattened out and the path widened. The party had come to a plateau, and on the far side, beyond a sheltering ledge of rock, the cliff sloped down to the beach and the water. Derrick told them to sit and rest while he scouted ahead.

"The cove is on the other side of those rocks, about thirty feet below us," Tom explained to Vi and Peter. "The cliff curves slightly here and pushes outward from the mountain, like an arm stretched to the ocean. The cove is formed inside the curve of the cliff."

"You have been here before," Peter remarked.

"When I was much younger," Tom said. "But it's not a good place. The beach is rocky and desolate, and the water's rough."

"The governor told Mark that it is impossible for a boat to get into the cove," Vi said. "Sir George said the bay is blocked by rocks and reefs."

Tom looked at her curiously. "There is a reef, but it is not impassable. A skilled fisherman can navigate it," he said.

Derrick returned a few minutes later, and he had news.

"There are men on the beach," he said in a hushed tone. "I counted a dozen. They have two flat-bottomed boats, and they're unloading crates. There's a ship anchored offshore, beyond the reef—a schooner. I'd say those men are smugglers, for sure."

"Did you see my husband?" Vi asked hopefully.

"No, ma'am," Derrick replied. "But the cave's at the base of the cliff, almost straight down from here. It's above the water line, and I saw men taking crates inside. If they have your husband, my guess is that he's there."

"Then we must get him out!" Vi exclaimed.

Derrick put a finger to his lips, and Vi instantly regretted her outburst.

"We need to keep quiet, Mrs. Raymond. Wind's up, and voices carry," Derrick cautioned. "There are too many men down there now for us to take on. We've got five men. They've got twelve, maybe more, and I figure they're armed. But I suspect most of the men will go back to the schooner when they've unloaded."

"They'll leave guards," said Tom.

"No more than four or five," Derrick responded with a wry smile. "Evens out the odds. We don't have weapons except our knives and machetes, but if we wait till dark, we can surprise them, and, God willing, no one will be hurt."

Thoughtfully, Tom said, "If they have the professor, they must know someone is looking for him, but they probably think we're searching the jungle. They might figure that we've sent to Georgetown for help from the army. But they won't expect soldiers for another couple of days at least, and by then they plan to be gone. We have a good chance of surprising them tonight."

"We have to succeed tonight," Vi said, keeping her voice low. "I have had the feeling since Elijah told his story that whoever took Mark did so deliberately. Please don't think me foolish. But why else would they have allowed Elijah to escape? If they wanted to keep their presence here secret, why did they not pursue him? I believe they *wanted* us to know that Mark was kidnapped."

Tom thought that Vi had a good point. "If they were trying to hide their illegal activities," he said, "they wouldn't have let the boy get away. It's possible they made it easy for Elijah to get loose of his bonds and run away. But why would they want the professor?"

"Ransom," Vi said.

"Ransom?" Derrick questioned. "Is your husband a rich man?"

Vi's jaw tightened. "No, he isn't rich. But my family is."

"Who besides you and your family would know that?" Tom asked.

"Just three people—Dr. Hockingham, Governor Dibbley, and Mr. Wigham," Vi replied. "And Dr. Hockingham is above all suspicion."

"Who's Mr. Wigham?" Tom asked.

"A peculiar young man who is private secretary to the governor. He has acted strangely since we met him, and he knows about the camp and the cove. He was in a meeting with my husband and the governor when they discussed the excavation and studied the map."

"You don't suspect the governor, do you?"

Vi didn't reply, but her mind was churning. *Why not the governor?* she thought. *Sir George knew a great deal—too much—about me and Mrs. O'Flaherty when we first met him. He*

has the resources of his office and the British government to investigate visitors to the island. He could easily have learned about the wealthy Dinsmore family. Is he involved with the smugglers? But he is wealthy himself. Would he risk his title and his reputation? Would he risk imprisonment? Why would the governor be so foolhardy?

Her suspicions, however, were focused on Mr. Wigham. As the governor's secretary, she realized, he had access to information and could just as easily have learned about her family's wealth as the governor could. She recalled her conversation with Mr. Wigham on the veranda of the governor's house. *What was that verse he quoted? 'Your enemy the devil prowls around like a roaring lion looking for someone to devour.' I thought he was talking about the mountain, perhaps warning us about its dangers. But what if he meant it as a threat? Could he be the devil who prowls? Was he counting on my remembering what he said? Was he trying to let me know that he is dangerous?*

Vi knew she was making rash assumptions and had no evidence to support them. But with her husband likely being held prisoner in a cave somewhere below where she stood, she didn't care. Someone had tried to take him from her and from their children. She clenched her hands into fists, and at that moment, she determined that whoever the kidnapper was, he would face man's justice just as surely as God's.

"It doesn't matter now who is at fault," she said at last. Her voice was calm and steely. "The mountain is casting long shadows, so night approaches. We must make our plan."

CHAPTER

11

Attempting an Ambush

The swift cannot flee nor the strong escape.

JEREMIAH 46:6

*T*hey ate the last of their cold food as they developed the plan. The men naturally assumed that Mrs. Raymond would remain in safe hiding, but Vi quickly corrected that notion. She would go with them, and she would help. Promising to follow Tom's and Derrick's instructions, she won their grudging acceptance.

One of the villagers went farther down the cliff to keep watch over the cove. As the sun was setting on the opposite side of the mountain, he returned to report that the two boats had left, carrying nine of the smugglers. The other three had built a fire on the rocky beach, and two more smugglers had come out of the cave.

"They're laughing and carrying on. I think they've got a good supply of rum," the villager said. "By the time the moon's high, they won't be able to put up such a good fight. A couple of 'em came down close to the water, not far from me, and I heard 'em joking about the man in the cave. One of 'em said, 'He's worth more 'n ten shiploads of contraband guns and stolen goods. The boss was right. A rich wife will pay a pretty penny to get her man back, she will.' "

Mark is there! Vi thought. She had been worrying about putting the others in jeopardy if they were wrong about Mark being held captive. She knew she would never forgive herself if any of the men with her was hurt. She had prayed for God to protect them all, even the smugglers. But now there was no doubt about the mission. If they failed— *No! I will not contemplate such a possibility.*

The men were going over the details of the plan again, and Vi turned her attention to their hushed conversation.

They would wait for about two hours to make their move. The moon would be high then, so they could descend the cliff safely and silently. The way down to the beach, Tom said, was much easier than their climb up the cliff.

Peter and a villager stretched out on the rocky ground to sleep. Tom leaned against a rock and nodded off. The villager who had been keeping watch also fell asleep. Before he left to take up the watch, Derrick kindly advised Vi to get some rest as well.

Vi settled against a boulder and tried to make herself comfortable. She closed her eyes, but sleep was no friend to her that night. The knowledge that Mark was so close taunted her, and her fears for him welled up inside her. The faces of Max, Lulu, and Gracie swam before her, and tears ran down her cheeks. For the first time since she had seen Elijah lying on the ground in camp, she felt her resolve weakening and her fear growing as images of her family filled her mind.

Then something inside her seemed to whisper, "Don't be afraid; just believe." She had so often quoted those words from the Book of Mark to the children, and now the words brought comfort to her. "Don't be afraid; just believe," she whispered to herself, and her fear began to melt.

She must have dozed off, for she woke with a start. A hand was shaking her shoulder. Looking up, she made out Tom's face in the moonlight. "It's time, Mrs. Raymond," he said.

Vi was instantly alert.

Attempting an Ambush

The rescue party set out, moving in single file down the cliff to the beach. The native men were nimble and quick, but Vi and Peter progressed more cautiously lest their steps loosen so much as a pebble that might tumble down the cliff and reveal their presence. When they reached the beach, Vi felt the rough rocks, made slippery in the tide, through the leather soles of her boots. The half moon had risen high enough to illuminate their way down the cliff and transform the waves of the sea into moving ribbons of quicksilver that broke into glittering fragments when the water reached the shore. But its light did not penetrate the upper portion of the beach. The only light came from the smugglers' fire, which glowed and crackled ominously and cast weird shadows on the overhanging cliff. *Tom said it was not a good place*, Vi thought, *and he was right*.

"They won't see our approach in this gloom," Tom whispered. "Stay close to the cliff and take care of your footing. When we reach the cave, you hang back, Mrs. Raymond. Derrick and his men will take the smugglers at the fire. Peter, you and I will handle anyone who comes out of the cave."

Still in single-file formation, the men and Vi crept forward. With every step, Vi prayed that her foot would hold fast. Then, as if at some secret signal, they stopped, and the three villagers broke away. They moved out onto the dark beach and toward the smugglers' fire. Vi became aware of a pale light, as from an oil lamp, just in front of where she, Tom, and Peter stood. As her eyes adjusted, she realized that this second light was coming from inside the cliff. *The cave!*

Tom whispered something in Peter's ear. Then the stalwart guide unwound the rope from his waist and handed one end to Peter. Crouching low, Tom moved across the cave opening to the opposite side. Peter gently pushed Vi against the cliff wall and whispered, "Stay here." Then he crouched down, and the two men pulled the rope tight across the cave entrance.

Vi held her breath. *Don't be afraid; just believe.*

From the direction of the fire came a dull thud. Then another. Someone yelled, but the yell was almost immediately stilled by yet another thud. There was the sound of someone running on the rocks. Vi heard a second set of feet scrambling on the beach. There was a high-pitched shout of "Nay!" followed by an explosive whack and another thud.

Everything went quiet for a moment, until a male voice echoed within the cave: "What was that noise?" A second voice commanded, "Go and see. Hurry!"

A man ran out of the mouth of the cave, and there was just enough light for Vi to see him hit the rope, lurch forward, and, with his arms thrown wide, fly into the dark. Peter jumped up and lunged for the man.

A second man ran from the cave, and Tom leapt up, grabbing the man and grappling him down onto the rocks. Tom and Peter both disappeared into the darkness with their adversaries.

Vi didn't know what to do, but at the sound of curses coming from within the cave, she moved. Her heart was pounding, but her legs were steady as she slipped around the opening of the cave. The deep shadows concealed her, but a thin light farther back in the cave allowed her to quickly scan the low space. The cave was stacked with rough wooden crates, and near the rear, she saw Mark seated on one of the boxes. She bit her lip to keep from calling out to him. He was blindfolded. His feet were tied with rope and his arms were stretched behind his back. The lamp was on a crate close to where he sat.

Attempting an Ambush

A tall man moved into the lamplight and leaned close to Mark's face. The man's back was to Vi, so she couldn't see his face, but she could hear his voice. It was rough and cruel when he said, "Do not think you will escape me, Professor Raymond. Your rescuers, if any are coming for you, are still more than a day away. In the old days, I would have slit your throat and thrown you to the sharks. But I will spare you, and if you are a lucky man, someone will find you here before you perish. Meanwhile, I shall be enjoying the ransom that your pretty wife will pay to have her treasure back."

From outside came a loud scream, and the tall man cursed again. "What are those blasted idiots doing?" he hissed, turning his head toward the cave entrance.

Vi sank into the shadows where he could not see her. But she could see him. His face was covered with a black hood!

"You wait here, Professor," the man said in the same low and hateful tone. "But, of course, you have no choice, do you? Not when you are tied up like a goat before the slaughter."

The hooded man strode to the cave entrance and drew a long saber from his belt. He looked into the darkness and quickly stepped back. He whispered something under his breath. Vi couldn't make out what he said, but she was certain it was another of his vile curses. The man was only about ten feet away from where she stood, and she dared not move a muscle. She was no match for a saber. *Where are the others?* she thought wildly. *Where is Tom?*

The man wore a dark cloak, which he now pulled about him. Vi watched as he pressed himself against the wall, and quickly darted out of the cave, slithering like a lizard over a hot stone.

183

She ran to Mark and pulled the blindfold from his eyes.

Blinking against the light, he struggled to focus on her face. "Vi, is that you?" he asked in a cracked voice.

She flung her arms around him and hugged him to her. She never wanted to let him go.

Vi was too intent on Mark to hear new shouts and cries coming from the beach. Tom called out, "Get him, Peter!" There was running and more shouting and finally the noise of a struggle. A single pair of booted feet ran over the rocks, followed by a metallic noise that Vi would have recognized if she had been listening. It was the sound of wooden oars locking into iron braces on the gunwales of a boat. Someone was getting away.

Weeping and laughing with joy, Vi at last broke her grasp and began to untie her husband. She had just freed Mark's hands when Derrick came into the cave. He rushed to where Mark sat and started to remove the rope around his ankles. "Good to see you, Professor. Did they hurt you, sir?"

"Just my pride," Mark said, his voice thick and hoarse from lack of water.

Vi held her canteen to Mark's lips, and he drank greedily. When he thanked her, he sounded nearly himself again.

"Elijah?" he asked. "Did you find him?"

"He found us," Vi replied. "He stumbled into camp just before daybreak. He had broken his arm and was exhausted, but he told us what happened. We sent him to Georgetown with Dr. Hockingham and Lorenzo. Elijah was very brave, and I am sure he will recover."

"But you should have gone with him," Mark said with concern.

"And leave you?" she laughed. "You know me better than that, my love."

He smiled at her—the slightly lopsided smile that always delighted her—and he wanted to take her into his embrace. But his arms were numb.

"Give me that rope, missus," Derrick said. "One of those scoundrels fled. Musta had another boat hidden on the other side of the cove. But we've got six of 'em. I can use these ropes to tie 'em down tight for the night."

"Was anyone hurt?" Vi asked.

"None of us, but the enemy's going home with their fair share of lumps and bruises," Derrick answered as he undid the last knot in Mark's bonds. "A couple were knocked out cold, but they'll be all right soon enough. Right enough for a long time in jail."

Derrick wasn't completely correct when he said no one had been hurt. Tom came into the cave a few minutes later, supporting Peter by the waist. Peter's shirt sleeve was torn and bloody, but he wore a huge grin on his face.

"I didn't count on him having a sword," Peter said as Tom helped him sit on a crate and then began to inspect his arm. "I had him pinned down until he swiped me with his blade and broke my hold. But I landed two or three good blows. His jaw's going to ache tomorrow."

"Did you get a good look at him?" Mark asked.

"No, sir," Peter replied, "for I tackled him in the shadows, and he had something over his face. Did you see who he was?"

"I was blindfolded the entire time," Mark said, shaking his head with regret. "I suppose he was the leader."

"Likely so," Tom agreed. "The men we captured all appear to be common seamen. I know one of them. He's a bad lot who hangs around the wharfs in Georgetown. If this group had a leader, then he's the one that got away."

Saying that Peter's wound was not deep, Tom cleaned it with some rum the kidnappers hadn't consumed and used Vi's headscarf to bandage it. Mark stood up slowly on his stiff legs, but he was soon walking as normally as ever and very glad to be at liberty after two days of captivity.

Tom, Derrick, and the village men brought their prisoners, all of whose hands were tied, into the cave and made them sit on the ground. Vi and Tom checked each man and ascertained that none of them was seriously injured. Tom then questioned the six kidnappers, but he got little information in return.

They found some food and water in the cave, and the rescuers ate. Then Derrick said he would take first watch while his companions slept. "I doubt we'll have any problems with our captives," he said with confidence. "They had a good bit of rum before we ambushed 'em, and they'll be sleeping it off."

The rescuers made themselves as comfortable as they could, and soon only Derrick and Tom remained awake. They talked in low voices.

"That all went right well," Derrick said. "I was worried about Mrs. Raymond—afraid she'd slow us down. But not a bit of it. She's a plucky young lady, Tom."

"Yes, I agree," Tom replied. "Mrs. Raymond's strong-willed in a good way. I was surprised to hear about her rich family. The way she was at camp, so hardworking and ready to learn—well, that wasn't like any pampered rich woman I ever saw. But, Derrick, there's one thing that's puzzling to me."

"No rain?" Derrick said.

"No rain," Tom affirmed. "Leastways, no rain down here on the shore tonight. The sky was clear, and that made it easy for us to get down the cliff and overwhelm those men. If they'd all been inside this cave, like they would have been if the rain was pouring, we'd have had a bad time of it. They have guns in here, and they would have used them. We might not have got the professor back in such good condition."

Derrick thought about this for some moments. Then he said, "It happens sometimes, Tom, nights without the rain. But not often. I guess we got lucky tonight."

"I don't believe in luck," Tom said. "I believe our Savior was with us. He protected Elijah and brought him back to the camp. That was like a miracle, Derrick, because the boy must have been scared nearly out of his wits. He could have run off in any direction and got himself well and truly lost. Elijah doesn't know the jungle, yet he came back by the straight way, in the dark of night. I know you were following his signs on the trail today. I believe the Lord was at Elijah's side. And I believe He held back the rain. Do you know Psalm 28?"

"Not so's I can quote it, my friend," Derrick said.

"There's a verse I keep in my heart," Tom said, "for times of trouble. 'The LORD is my strength and my shield; my heart trusts in him.' "

"That's a right good verse," Derrick said. "Say it again for me, will you, so I can remember it."

The return trip to the camp took a full day and most of the night, primarily because the prisoners were unused to overland travel and were very slow. Having slept off their alcoholic binge, they were also full of complaints about the treatment they had received from the rescuers. The smugglers were seamen, and the jungle frightened and unnerved them. They had to be watched constantly, lest one of them veer away from the cleared trail and become lost. "You boys make a sorry bunch of pirates," Derrick called out in annoyance. "Can't even find your way through the woods!"

Even Vi, who had sympathy for their aches and pains, grew tired of the smugglers' constant carping and lagging. When they at last reached the camp, she was greatly relieved to find Colonel McTyiere and a contingent of soldiers there, sitting around the campfire with Liberty.

The soldiers took custody of the prisoners, putting them under arrest. It was agreed that the prisoners would be transported in the large wagon belonging to the expedition team and that the soldiers would leave one of their horses behind. The British colonel informed Mark and Vi that Elijah was doing well and that he and Dr. Hockingham were staying in the American consul's house.

"The older fellow wanted to come with us," Colonel McTyiere told Mark, "but I convinced him otherwise."

Mark smiled and said, "I am sure Dr. Hockingham is eager to return to our dig."

"You have found something interesting?" the colonel inquired.

"We may have, but we do not know yet," Mark said. "If you should see Dr. Hockingham before I get to Georgetown, please assure him that he will be back at work soon."

"I will report to him myself," the colonel promised, "as soon as we have these miscreants locked in the stockade. They have committed crimes against the British crown —

smuggling, gun running, abduction for ransom—and they shall be punished. I will need a formal statement from you, Professor Raymond, but it can await your return. Are you quite certain you do not wish to come with us? We can guarantee you safe convoy."

Mark glanced at Vi, and in the light of the fire, he saw the weariness in her face. He too could not bear the thought of making the ride before they rested, so he politely declined the colonel's offer.

"I don't believe we are in any danger now," Mark said. "We also need to secure the camp before we leave. We will set out early tomorrow, after a good night's sleep."

"I shall tell Lady Jane that," the colonel said. "Governor Dibbley has been away for the last week, so he knows nothing of this matter. But Lady Jane has been very concerned. She wanted you to know that your children and your friend are fine, and that the children are unaware of your difficulty. Do you have any message for her?"

"Just tell Lady Jane that we will be there very soon," Vi said, "and thank her for her kindness to the children and Mrs. O'Flaherty."

As soon as the sun came up, the soldiers and their prisoners departed, accompanied by the men of the village. Mark insisted that Vi retire to their tent and sleep. She did not argue; in truth, she was exhausted. Now that Mark was out of danger and the adventure was behind them, the full realization of what *might* have happened struck her. The physical and emotional stress of the past three days overwhelmed her body, and she dropped onto her cot with great relief.

Spreading a light blanket over her, Mark kissed his wife tenderly and said, "You are my heroine, my dear and determined wife. Were you ever afraid?"

"Only for you," she said sleepily. "But even then, I trusted God."

"Close your eyes now," he said. He touched her forehead and gently brushed back some tangled strands of her thick dark hair. Then he bent and kissed her again and knew that she was already asleep.

He was spreading the netting around her when a bit of Shakespeare came to him: "O sleep! O gentle sleep! Nature's soft nurse…"

Sleep well, my love, he thought as he reluctantly left Vi's side. *God has brought us through this trial, but it is not at an end yet. There is still a piece left to the puzzle. Lord, please grant me the wisdom to find the truth and the strength to control my anger when I find the man responsible for this. Help me to do what is right and just and merciful, in Your name.*

Unmasking the Lion

Therefore judge nothing before the appointed time; wait till the Lord comes. He will bring to light what is hidden in darkness and will expose the motives of men's hearts.

1 CORINTHIANS 4:5

*M*ark and Vi arrived at the governor's compound very late the next night and went straight to the guest house. They had decided not to wake the sleeping household, so the young Raymonds had been happily surprised to find their parents waiting to have breakfast with them. The children's first questions were about the expedition, and Mark quickly explained what had been found so far.

When Lulu asked if anything really exciting had occurred, Mark told them the story of the kidnapping and the rescue. He made a point of keeping his tone light, so not to frighten his children. But when he had finished, Gracie exclaimed: "He might have killed you, Papa! That terrible kidnapper man in the hood might have *killed* you! We have to thank Jesus that you and Mamma weren't hurt. Please, may we say a prayer and thank our Lord for bringing you home to us?"

Their family prayer was especially precious to them all, and their gratitude to their Heavenly Friend and Protector was enormous. Each expressed his or her thanks for the happy outcome of the search and the rescue, and Gracie added a plea that the soldiers would capture the hooded man "so he can't kidnap anyone ever again."

Assured that their parents were no longer in danger, the inquisitive young Raymonds were so full of questions that Vi and Mrs. O had to remind them repeatedly to eat. Finally, Mark laughed cheerfully and said, "If you three will finish your breakfast with no more questions, I will declare a holiday from lessons today. Then you may pester me as much as you want, and I shall enjoy every minute of it."

The children thought this was a very good bargain. They finished their meal, and then Mark took them for a walk to see the horses in the governor's stable. This gave Vi a chance to speak with Mrs. O'Flaherty and Beatrice. She learned that her note had been delivered to Lady Jane in the governor's absence and that Lady Jane had gone by herself to the military garrison to summon help.

"Wasn't Mr. Wigham here?" Vi inquired. "Was he with the governor?"

"He wasn't here when Abraham arrived with your message," Mrs. O'Flaherty said, "but he wasn't with the governor either."

"I think Sir George had sent Mr. Wigham out to one of the plantations," Beatrice said. "The governor doesn't often take Mr. Wigham on his long trips. Mr. Wigham came back yesterday, and the governor's expected later today."

"Does Sir George often take long trips?" Vi asked.

Beatrice considered for a moment. "Now that I think about it, Sir George goes off on his own fairly frequently. Maybe every month or so, he's away for a week or more, and he usually goes alone. To tell the truth, Mrs. Raymond, the house servants look forward to his and Mr. Wigham's absences. The governor's not as popular with those who work for him as he is with other folks. And Mr. Wigham is just so strange and secretive. Nobody complains, though, out of respect for her ladyship."

"And how is Lady Jane?" Vi asked.

"Very worried about you and the professor," Beatrice said. "Since she got your note and sent off the soldiers to find you, she's spent most of her time by herself. Cook had to make her ladyship take meals. I'm sure she was very relieved when Colonel McTyiere came with the news that you were safe and the kidnappers were locked up."

Not all the kidnappers, Vi thought. "I should go to the main house now and see Lady Jane," she said. "I want to thank her."

"Do you want me to accompany you?" asked Mrs. O.

"No," Vi replied. "You wait for Mark and the children. I was thinking we might arrange a visit to the beach this afternoon — the one Mr. Featherstone took us to on our first sightseeing trip. Will you see if that is agreeable to Mark?"

Mrs. O'Flaherty walked with Vi to the door of the house, while Beatrice cleared the table. Beyond the young maid's earshot, Mrs. O said, "You have something on your mind, Vi girl."

Vi smiled and took her friend's hand. "And you are much too observant," she responded. "I may be awhile with Lady Jane, so don't be concerned," she added, hurrying down the porch steps and toward the governor's residence.

Vi was ushered into Lady Jane's upstairs sitting room and immediately greeted with an embrace. "I am so glad you are here," Lady Jane said. "I have missed you."

Lady Jane stepped back and looked at Vi. "You appear in good health," her ladyship said with a warm smile. "The sun has tanned you, and it is very attractive. Is Professor Raymond equally well?"

"He is," Vi said. "He is much tanner than I and no worse for wear after his ordeal. I am so grateful to you for your assistance. I am not sure how we would have managed the smugglers we caught if you had not dispatched the soldiers so quickly."

Motioning Vi to a chair, Lady Jane took her seat. "Do you mind if I ask some questions?" she asked. "I don't want to tire you."

Noticing that it was Lady Jane who appeared tired, her pretty face drawn and pale, Vi replied, "I would be glad to tell you anything you'd like to know. Perhaps if I begin with a summary of the events…"

"Please, do," Lady Jane agreed.

For the next five minutes, Vi told the story, though without the many exciting details that Mark had supplied for the children. When she finished, her ladyship questioned her closely about the kidnappers, particularly the leader.

"Can you describe the man in the hood?" Lady Jane began.

"Not really, except to say that he was tall."

"But you heard his voice. Could you recognize it?"

"I don't think so. It was a gruff voice, but muffled by the hood. Mark thinks the man was disguising his voice, making himself sound rough and crude. He did have an English accent."

"English? Not Scots or Irish or a native accent?"

"I'm sure it was English, and Mark thinks so as well. I really wish I could tell you more," Vi said regretfully, "but I barely saw the man and only heard him speak a few words. Mark was blindfolded the entire time and didn't see him at all. Not even Peter Andersen, the young man who fought with him in the darkness, saw the hooded man's face."

Lady Jane sat back and sighed. Her expression was pensive.

"Perhaps it will be possible to learn more from the prisoners," Vi suggested.

"Colonel McTyiere tells me they have revealed very little under his initial interrogation. They claim to be innocent seamen who know nothing about the illegal guns and rum you found in the cave," said Lady Jane with an ironic smile. "One of them did say that they had a man on the beach who saw your husband there, but that is all. Thus far, the prisoners are being very loyal to their leader. They even say that there was no seventh man on the beach that night—no hooded man. From what you have told me, Vi, I believe that you were the only person, aside from the smugglers, to get a clear look at the man."

Vi, who had not thought of this before, nodded in agreement.

"Is there any detail about him that you remember, my dear, anything that might distinguish him?" Lady Jane asked in an urgent manner.

Vi closed her eyes and summoned up the scene in the cave. She saw Mark again, tied up and blindfolded. She saw the lamp casting its low light. She saw the man coming into view. He was tall, yes, with broad shoulders and a strong build. His hair was black—no—the hood covered his head, and it was black. In her mind's eye, the man seemed to be dressed head to foot in black. She moved the scene forward in her imagination. The man looking up when he heard the sounds from outside the cave, the man approaching the entrance. He was turned slightly in her direction. He was doing something. She could see his hand go to his belt and—

"He was wearing a wide brown leather belt," Vi said. "I can see it. He took a saber from his belt. It glinted in the light. It was silver with a gold hilt! Something flashed when he stepped back into the cave—a jewel of some sort. It was red! A red ruby!"

Vi's eyes flew open. "I can see it now!" she exclaimed excitedly. "The curved, silvery steel blade. The gold handle. And a large ruby on the guard that shields the handle. How could I have forgotten?"

"This is important information," said Lady Jane, who had caught Vi's excitement. "We must get this news to Colonel McTyiere. I will call for Mr. Wigham. He can write up an account of your evidence."

"Let me find him," Vi said, rising from her chair.

"He is probably in his office," Lady Jane said. "Go into Sir George's office and through the door on your left."

Vi went down the stairs and to a door she hadn't entered before. There was a small bronze plaque on the door that read: "Sir George Dibbley." She went in, and as she expected, the room was empty. Going to the door on the left, she knocked. There was no answer. She rapped again, but still no response. She opened the door and saw that no one was there. Mr. Wigham's office was hardly bigger than a closet and had only one, narrow window set high on the wall. There was a lamp burning, and several open files lay scattered on the desktop, telling her that Mr. Wigham had not gone for long. She stepped back into the governor's office to wait for the officious secretary.

Looking about the governor's large and elegantly appointed room, she thought what a contrast it was to the cramped space Mr. Wigham occupied. Her eyes went over the room is a desultory way, seeing but not really taking in more than impressions of the large polished desk, the paintings and set of swords on the wall, the British flag on a standard, the leather-bound books on some shelves. She was wondering if it was wise to confide her new information to Mr. Wigham. But as she conjured up the image of the tall, reed-thin secretary with the tenor voice, she suddenly knew that he could not have been the man in the hood. *The man in the cave was bigger and stronger, and his voice was deep. Mr. Wigham could not have disguised himself so completely. Yet he may have played some role in the kidnapping*, she thought.

Deciding that she still could not trust Mr. Wigham, Vi returned to Lady Jane and made an alternate proposal.

"I couldn't find Mr. Wigham," Vi said, "but I have a better plan. I am going back to the guest house for my sketchbook and pencils. I will draw a picture of the man I saw in the cave. That will be more useful than a written description, don't you think, Lady Jane?"

"Much better," Lady Jane replied with an expression that Vi could not interpret. "Bring your drawing to me when you complete it, and I will get it to Colonel McTyiere."

Vi excused herself and was hurrying down the stairs when something occurred to her. She stood still, gripping the banister tightly and forcing her mind to work. *I have seen something this morning*, she thought, *something important. What was it? Think, Vi Raymond, think!*

She sat down on the step and closed her eyes. She would do what she had done to remember the appearance of the hooded man in the cave. She began to form pictures in her mind of every place she had been and everything she had done that morning. She visualized the guest house, but nothing unusual struck her. She envisioned the path to the main house, then Lady Jane's sitting room. Except for Lady Jane's wan face, Vi could not see anything of particular note. Her mind traveled to the governor's office and slowly scanned its décor. The massive desk, the flag behind it, the bookshelves, a portrait of some man in military uniform, a set of watercolor paintings of battle scenes, two swords mounted on the wall, a marble bust on a stand, a—

Wait! Go back. Vi mentally reviewed the room and settled her vision on the swords.

Opening her eyes, she stood up and ran down the steps and along the hallway. Flinging open the door to the governor's office, she went directly to where the swords hung—two highly polished swords resting one above the other on metal brackets secured to the wall. She also saw what she now expected. There was a third set of brackets beneath the two swords. On her previous visit to the office, she remembered, the brackets had been empty. Now, they cradled a sword with a curved blade and an intricately etched golden hilt. But there was something odd. The saber was laid in the opposite direction from the two swords above it.

Carefully, Vi reached for the saber. It was heavy, but she was able to shift its position just enough so that she could see the opposite side of the hilt, which had been hidden against the wall. She gasped softly. A bright, red gem was set in the handle.

"Do you like my saber, Mrs. Raymond?" came a man's voice behind her. "It is said to have belonged to the great General Napoleon Bonaparte himself."

With a quick prayer asking the Lord for strength, Vi slipped the saber back into its place. Squaring her shoulders, she turned slowly and said, "It is a beautiful weapon. I did not get so close a view on first seeing it, Sir George."

The governor was standing on the opposite side of the room, his back to a window. With the sunlight behind him, he appeared to be in silhouette, like a black paper cutting. Vi realized that he must have been in the room the whole time. She glanced at the door to the hall. She had left it open, but now it was shut.

"I polish those swords myself," Sir George said in an amiable tone that made Vi's blood run cold. "The servants and even my wife know never to touch them. A wise precaution. Too bad I did not warn you to keep your pretty hands off. Too bad I underestimated your powers of observation. I stopped at the garrison and spoke with Colonel McTyiere before coming here. He told me of your presence at the cave. He spoke very highly of your courage, by the way."

"That was kind of him," Vi said, keeping her voice even. "I did suspect that the man in the hood might be you, but I prayed that I was wrong, for Lady Jane's sake."

"Ah, yes, my wife," said the governor. He moved toward his desk, and Vi could see his face now. He looked no different from the way he had when she first met him. Nothing in his face or his posture indicated who he really was.

"I am sure you are thinking that Lady Jane deserves better than me," he said.

"Yes, I think she deserves much better than a smuggler and a kidnapper," Vi replied. She didn't move her gaze from his face, but if she could inch her way toward the door, she would be able to make her escape. *I have to keep him talking*, she thought. *As long as he is talking about himself, he may not notice my movement.*

"But you do not understand, Mrs. Raymond," he said. "My activities—my sideline business, you might say—are what keep her in this house she loves so much. Her family owned Gilead, you know, for four generations. But her father was a terrible businessman, and a downturn in the sugar market nearly ruined him. I was able to purchase the plantation and save the poor man and his family from bankruptcy. I even agreed to allow him to keep this house and the grounds, including the guest house. He died soon after our transaction, and my wife inherited the place. We were all living in London at the time, and Lady Jane was regarded as quite a catch among the young aristocrats. Every popinjay with a title was courting her, but I—a mere commoner, the son of a tavern owner—won her hand. I had saved her father from disgrace. She was young, and I am sure she mistook her gratitude for love."

Vi had taken several tiny steps as he talked. "But you had wealth, and wealth earned you a title," she said. "What has caused you to turn to theft and abduction?"

He smiled, relaxing against the edge of his desk, and said, "I could tell you it was a love of adventure, a mad desire to live the life of a buccaneer. Most women would sympathize with romantic poppycock of that sort. But I do not believe you are the sentimental type. The truth is that my manufacturing business in England fell on hard times some years ago, and I was forced to sell to a competitor before I lost everything. I used my connections—the politicians who had secured my title—to get the governorship of the islands. I intended to let Her Majesty's government pay for my stay here while I rebuilt my fortune on sugar. There will always be a demand for sugar. Unfortunately, the Caribbean must now compete with the United States and Europe and other parts of the world. Do you know, Mrs. Raymond, that they even produce sugar in Scandinavia? From beets. I have managed to transfer funds from my official budget to my own accounts, but not nearly enough to cover my debts. The simple answer to your question is that I needed money, and I discovered that smuggling was far more lucrative than sugar cane."

"So you are an embezzler as well, stealing from your own government," Vi said. "Does Lady Jane know any of this?"

"Very little," he replied. "There was one occasion when someone almost exposed my activities to her, but she would not believe ill of me."

And that someone was Henry Featherstone! Vi thought in a flash.

"Returning here to Gilead has made her happy," Sir George continued, "and I see no reason to involve my wife, or any woman, in matters of finance."

He looked down at his desk, and Vi took another sideways step toward her objective, the door.

Without looking up, Sir George said harshly, "It is locked, Mrs. Raymond."

Vi felt panic rising in her, but she fought it back. *Surely he will not harm me—not here.* Controlling herself, she asked, "Why have you told me all this?"

"Because I respect your intellect," he responded mildly, "and I know you can appreciate a good offer when you hear it. I admit that my ransom plan against your husband was too melodramatic. I did guess correctly, however, that warning the professor away from the cove would arouse his curiosity. I was aboard the schooner when he and the other fellow found the cave and were spotted by one of my men. It was easy to capture them and arrange for the younger man to escape and inform you of the danger. I did not, however, account for your resolve, perhaps because I am unaccustomed to dealing with determined women. I assumed that you and that motley crew of scientists and locals would flee back to Georgetown for help. By ship, I would have been able to return here ahead of you and take charge of the search. I had planned to misdirect the searchers into the mountains. I believed the delay would have given plenty of time for my agents to have collected the ransom before anyone would have found your professor."

Unable to keep the bitterness out of her voice, Vi said, "And Mark would have likely died of thirst before he was found." Struggling to lighten her tone, she added, "Yet your grandiose scheme went wrong. You seem to have a pattern of failing when you are faced with opposition."

He slammed his fist upon the desk. "Do not mock me," he snarled. "Not when your family's safety is in the balance."

"What do you mean?"

"If you want your husband to continue his work here, if you want your children to enjoy the rest of their happy island idyll without any *unpleasant accidents*, I will make it happen — for a reasonable fee."

"A fee!" Vi exclaimed sarcastically. "Call it by its correct name — *extortion*. You want money in exchange for not harming my family."

"Calm yourself, Mrs. Raymond. You have plenty of money," Sir George said with an ugly grin. "You already share your wealth with the poor at that mission of yours. Just consider me another of your flock. If not me, consider my wife."

"Your wife would be horrified if she knew," Vi said. "And she will know. Everyone will know, for I will not accept your offer. I will see you in jail!"

"But who will believe your story?" he asked, moving toward Vi. "Where is your evidence?"

"*You* are the lion," she said without thinking. "You are the devil who prowls like a lion."

Sir George didn't seem to hear her. He continued his advance, and she backed against the wall, instinctively glancing sideways at the saber. He was now so close that she had to look up into his face, and he reached behind her, taking the saber from the wall.

"This is your evidence?" he asked, holding the weapon so that the ruby was just before her eyes. "This saber can vanish and easily be replaced by another. No one will ever know the difference, but they may doubt the sanity of a young woman who claims to have seen a ruby where none exists. Colonel McTyiere will assume that your recent and terrifying experience has temporarily unhinged your mind. He will never suspect me—the governor—of such atrocious behavior. How could he? I would have to be a madman to concoct such a plot. And plainly, I am not mad."

As he held the razor-sharp blade between them, Vi understood that he was not sane. She was trembling with fear, for she had no idea what to do and she was afraid to say anything more, lest her words should push him to violent action. *Don't be afraid; just believe*, she told herself in her desperation.

Suddenly, an arm darted around the governor's neck and someone grasped the hand holding the saber, twisting it until the governor yelped and dropped the weapon. It clattered to the floor, inches away from Vi's feet. Whoever was holding Sir George used one hand to force the governor's wrist down and around behind his back, all the while keeping his other arm around the governor's neck. Sir George tried to struggle, but the unknown person maintained a tight grip.

Vi was too stunned to move. Her eyes were riveted on the governor's contorted face. Sir George's cheeks bulged, and his color changed to a sickly purple. His eyes seemed to protrude from their sockets, and he struggled for breath.

"Don't kill him!" Vi shouted.

The arm released its hold, and gasping for air, the governor collapsed on the floor. Mr. Wigham stood over him.

"You!" Vi exclaimed.

Robert Wigham looked at her and grinned. "I am stronger than I appear, Mrs. Raymond. I was in my office when he and then you entered. I heard everything. Please, ma'am, would you ring that bell behind Sir George's desk? I may need some help to restrain him, and we must send to the garrison for assistance."

Vi ran to the bell cord and pulled it. She also remembered to unlock the office door. Within a minute, the butler, Rafe, came in. He was clearly confused, and at first he thought Mr. Wigham had attacked the governor.

Mr. Wigham took something from his breast pocket and handed it to the butler. "I am an agent of Her Majesty's Foreign Service," he said. "Sir George Dibbley is in my custody. I am relieving him of his official position as of now."

Rafe looked at the identification badge in his hand, then at Robert Wigham, and finally at the governor, who lay moaning and sputtering on the floor. He raised his gaze to Robert again and smiled wryly. "I'll go to the garrison myself," the butler said. "I'll have a couple of the gardeners come in to help you watch over Sir —" He stopped himself, cleared his throat, and finished his sentence by saying, "over this despicable criminal."

The butler dispatched a servant to find Professor Raymond and tell him to come to the governor's office. But he warned everyone else in the house not to mention the bizarre goings-on to Lady Jane.

When Mark entered the office, he was shocked to see Sir George slumped in a low chair, with two strong men standing on either side of him. Quickly and efficiently, Robert explained to Mark what had happened and that Sir George was the kidnapper.

"Where's Vi?" Mark demanded. "Is she unhurt?"

"She is really fine, sir," Robert said. "She got a fright, and I apologize for not intervening earlier. I have been trying to build a case against his lordship for months now. But Mrs. Raymond, well, she stood up to him for ten minutes and got a full confession. Your wife is a heroine, sir, and I am going to see that she is recognized for her bravery."

"But where is she?" Mark asked again.

"Upstairs, sir. She went to tell Lady Jane."

Mark took the hall steps two at a time. Reaching the landing, he turned to see Vi emerging from her ladyship's sitting room.

Seeing Mark, she ran into his arms. "It's all over, my darling," she said, as he smothered her face with kisses. "We're all safe now."

Mark could not believe what had happened. Just two hours earlier they had been at the breakfast table, telling their children of his kidnapping and rescue. Now his extraordinary wife had captured the mastermind of the plot. He wanted to know all the details, but Vi asked him to wait until later, when they could sort out the whole story together.

"Did you organize the trip to the beach?" Vi asked, looking up into his blue-gray eyes and flashing her dimpled smile, which Mark could never resist.

"Yes, but I'll cancel it," he said quickly.

"Oh, no, don't do that," Vi said, and Mark caught the look of mischief in her eyes.

"What are you up to now?" he wondered aloud.

"I have one more duty to perform before this puzzle is finally resolved," she said. "Besides, I think I have earned a relaxing afternoon at the seaside. Did you engage Mr. Featherstone to drive us?"

"I did," he said with a nod. "He will meet us in Georgetown at one thirty."

"That's perfect," she said. "Just perfect."

The family and Mrs. O'Flaherty met Mr. Featherstone at the Empire Hotel, and he conveyed them to the beach in his carriage. The sandy shore looked exactly the same as it had on their first visit. Mark, who had not been there before, was enchanted, and he and the children were soon in the water. Mrs. O'Flaherty, who had been told of Vi's mission, took a book and a towel and settled into a shady spot under the palm trees to read.

Henry Featherstone unhitched his horse while Vi watched.

"Aren't you going in the water, ma'am?" he asked.

"I want to talk to you first," Vi said, and she told him about the governor's arrest.

Shaking his head ruefully, Henry said, "I knew he was bad. That's why I left his service. But this—does Lady Jane know?"

"She is why I am here," Vi said. "She did not ask me to speak to you. I am taking that responsibility upon myself.

But she told me what caused the rift between you. I know that you found some irregularities in the governor's accounts when you were working for him. I know that you told Lady Jane of your suspicions. And I know that she refused to believe you."

"I didn't blame her for that," Henry said. "I was casting doubt on her husband, whom she trusted and cared for. She just couldn't see the greed in him, so I left because I didn't want to cause her trouble."

Vi took a deep breath of the clean sea air before she said, "Lady Jane sees it now. She has had doubts for a long time, but instead of facing them, she retreated. She told me that she avoided you, Mr. Featherstone, because she could not bear to be reminded of your suspicions. I believe you were her last real friend. She has been encased in a shell of fear, just like the sea creatures you showed us."

"She was outgoing as a child," Henry said sadly. "I worked for the family before they went back to England. It was her father who saw that I got good schooling. Did Lady Jane tell you that I taught her how to ride? She was a fearless little thing. Used to scare me half to death, watching how she'd gallop her pony off across the fields without a care for her own safety. But she was full of the joy of life then. I hate to think of her any other way."

"I believe that fearless child is still inside her," Vi said. "When I told her about Sir George, she made no excuses for him. She prayed for God's mercy on him, but she is deeply hurt by his betrayal of her trust. She also feels she has done you a great wrong, and she wants the chance to be forgiven and to make amends if she can."

Henry said, "I told her she has nothing to apologize to me for."

"She believes that she does," Vi responded, "and she *needs* the opportunity to ask for your forgiveness. If you still regard her as a friend, you can give her that. Will you help her, Mr. Featherstone, by being her friend again?"

Henry pondered this question deeply. "I've always been her friend really, but I haven't shown it," he said at last. "Let my pride get in the way. I want to make it up to her ladyship and to the Lord. You see, ma'am, I need forgiveness too."

"Would you be willing to drive us all the way back to Gilead today?" Vi asked.

"I would like to do just that," he replied with a smile. "Perhaps I'll have a word with Lady Jane while I'm there. Let her know I'm available if she has need of a driver."

"Or a friend," Vi said.

"That too," he answered. "That too."

Vi walked down to the ocean, shedding her shoes and stockings on the way.

"Look at me, Mamma!" shouted Gracie. The little girl, held securely in Mark's arms, was stretched out in the water on her stomach and kicking her legs wildly. "Papa's teaching me to swim!"

Vi waved and then clapped her hands in approval. She spotted Lulu and Max constructing a large sand fortress farther down the beach. Looking back toward the cliff, she saw that Mrs. O had fallen asleep with her book over her face.

Vi wiggled her toes in the wet sand. She closed her eyes and raised her face to the sun, enjoying the heat. She breathed in and out slowly and opened her ears to the soothing, rhythmic sound of the sea rushing in and going out again. She thought of Mark and the children safe and happy around her, and her loved ones back at home. Her mind was washed clean of worries, and she thanked God for the beauty and the glory of the moment. *Your faithful and unfailing love,* Vi prayed, *is the greatest of all Your gifts, dear Lord. You've allowed me to experience it on this earth through my family—I can only imagine what Your perfect and limitless love will be like when we enter into Your house in Heaven.* Vi looked out at Mark, Lulu, Max, and Gracie frolicking happily in the blue water and on the beach. *Oh, Heavenly Father, You have blessed my life with more than I could ever have asked or imagined.*

Epilogue

For you have been my hope,
O Sovereign LORD,
my confidence since
my youth.

PSALM 71:5

Epilogue

"No story ever has a perfect ending, but ours surely has a happy one," Mark said.

He and Vi were standing on the deck of the *Minerva*, looking out at the expanse of sea beneath the starry sky. Lulu, Gracie, and Max were sleeping peacefully in their cabin, and in the ship's lounge, Mrs. O'Flaherty was playing pinochle with a congenial group of passengers.

"I hope our adventure is not quite so challenging when we return to Christiana next year," Vi said in reply to her husband's observation.

"I have been intending to discuss that with you," Mark said, slipping his arm around her waist. "It would be selfish of me to expect the children to forgo three or four months of school every time I go on an expedition. And I know that you and Mrs. O'Flaherty have missed being away from the mission for so long. What do you think about my going back to Christiana next February and you and the children joining me for the month of May? You and the children can come to the excavation site for as long as you want."

"I think a month in May will be just right for all of us," Vi agreed.

"We will finish digging out the little temple, and I hope we can start on the site we located in the field near the cove. I think it may reveal a village of some size—evidence of ancient colonization."

Vi replied with a contented, "Umm," and rested her head against his shoulder.

Violet's Foreign Intrigue

The ship was taking them toward home, but her thoughts still lingered with the people of Christiana. It had been hard to say good-bye, especially to Lady Jane. But her ladyship had changed so much in the last two months that Vi had no doubts about her well-being. After Sir George was transported back to England for trial, Lady Jane had been transformed, like a butterfly leaving its cocoon. She had taken over the running of Gilead plantation and was determined to make it profitable once more. Her first act was to hire Mr. Featherstone as her manager, and he and his family were soon to move into the guest house.

Robert Wigham was still living at Gilead, for he had received a new assignment from the Foreign Office in London. He was to stay in Christiana and serve as acting governor until a new appointment could be made. He was not especially pleased with the job; he had no ambition to be a diplomat, but he would be able to continue his investigation into Sir George's criminal activities. Robert, whose real ambition was to leave the Foreign Service and become a Scotland Yard detective, believed he had a good chance of bringing the remainder of Sir George's band to justice and ending the smuggling trade on the island.

Dr. Hockingham and his two assistants had left the island several days ahead of the Raymonds. Elijah still had his arm in a sling, but he was resilient, and when Mark, Vi, and the others had returned to the dig, he had been with them. When Vi and Mark went to the wharf to bid their colleagues farewell, Vi noticed that Elijah was again wearing the braided leather bracelet they had found in the jungle. "You are a good friend," she whispered to Peter Andersen.

Epilogue

"I think I shall be a best man by Christmas," Peter replied, "now that Dr. Hockingham has given his approval for Elijah to marry."

They left one of their number behind. Malachi Bottoms had recuperated well under Dr. Cowden's and Mrs. Darling's care, but he was still not at his full strength and had decided not to make the voyage back to the United States. Vi had been concerned until Mrs. Darling confided that Malachi's health was not the primary reason for his decision.

"The boy has fallen in love with the island," Mrs. Darling had told Vi. "He is an artist, and I believe he's found his subject here. The paintings he is working on are nothing like his scientific work. The colors, Mrs. Raymond, are a glory to behold. Besides, it's done Dr. Cowden a world of good to have Malachi to talk to. And I don't much mind having Malachi around," she'd added in what Vi regarded as a masterpiece of understatement.

Vi had thought she might have to leave Mrs. O'Flaherty behind as well. With the kidnapping case solved, Mrs. O began spending more time with the vicar and his sister. Reverend Smythe had always wanted to set up a medical clinic, and he had a pledge of financial assistance from his church's missionary ministry. But the vicar had no head for organization, and every time he tried to make a plan, it ended in a muddle. Mrs. O'Flaherty was the answer to the churchman's frequent prayers for guidance. She knew not only what needed to be done but also how to do it. To everyone's astonishment, the chipper Mrs. Smiley had learned quickly from Mrs. O and displayed a hitherto unknown wealth of practical abilities. The project had moved forward rapidly, and Mrs. O'Flaherty wanted to see it through. But when the recruitment of physicians became an urgent problem, Mrs. O finally decided that she should go back to India Bay with the family and seek advice from Dr. Bowman.

"Considering all that had occurred in the last four months," Vi remarked, "you said our story has a happy ending, but I don't believe it is over."

Mark stroked his mustache and said, "I must agree. We have places to dig for new knowledge in all four corners of the world."

"And three very interesting children to raise at home," Vi noted.

"That's what really matters, my love," he said. "I never would have known the joy of being their father without you. Do you think we will ever become weary of being parents?"

"Oh, I hope not," Vi said in pretend shock. "Not until all our children are grown and ready to take on the world without us."

"I wonder what they will do with their lives," Mark said.

"Max has decided to follow in your footsteps," Vi replied.

"Has he really?" Mark said with undisguised pride. "So he has given up his aspirations to become a modern buccaneer?"

Vi laughed lightly and said, "The romance of piracy has been entirely replaced by the reality of archaeology in his imagination. And Lulu's current ambition is to become a geologist, for she says that is the best way for her to see distant lands. Gracie just wants to see Polly and Miss Moran and Kaki and to spend a quiet summer of play in India Bay."

Epilogue

"A quiet summer," Mark mused. "That sounds very good to me as well."

They decided to take one more walk about the ship before retiring.

"Which direction do you prefer, my lady? Aft or bow?" Mark asked chivalrously.

Vi thought for a moment. "To the bow, kind sir," she said, and Mark could hear the smile in her voice.

"Is there a particular reason for choosing the front of the ship?" he inquired.

"Oh, yes," she said, squeezing his arm gently. "Christiana is behind us for the time being. All our experiences there were good, even when they were difficult, because they taught us about ourselves and each other and they drew us closer than ever. The Bible tells us that 'everything that was written in the past was written to teach us,' and, my love, I learned many new lessons during our adventure in Christiana. Now I am ready to look forward, put what I've learned into practice, and try to be a better servant of the Lord."

"What do you want to make better?" Mark asked.

In the moonlight, he could not see her flush as she said, "I must learn not to judge others so readily. I can hardly forgive myself for suspecting Mr. Wigham based solely on his manner and his appearance."

"Well, he has certainly forgiven you for that error," Mark laughed. "In fact, he wants to give you a medal!"

"I know," Vi said. "And I know that the Lord forgives me. But each new day is a chance for me, for all of us, to improve ourselves and do better for Him with the help of His Holy Spirit."

They had reached the front of the ship. Mark put his arm around his wife and held her close. The ship plowed through the shiny sea, and they sensed the forward motion in the hum of the engines below their feet and the touch of the night wind on their faces.

"I keep thinking of something my Cousin Molly told me a long time ago," Vi said in a soft and gentle tone. "It was just before her marriage to Mr. Embery, and I was very sad at the thought of being separated from her. I was also afraid of growing up and of all the changes and challenges that awaited me in the future. Molly taught me not to be fearful. I remember her exact words: 'Every day of our lives—even in hardship and trials—we are growing toward God.'"

There, on the prow of a ship steaming a steady course toward home, Vi and Mark both felt these words in their hearts. Like the vast ocean, their future spread out before them, full of possibilities, and their love for the Lord and for each other and their children would strengthen them for whatever storms lay ahead. Together, they would grow in faith and love.

With a dimpled smile and a voice golden with hope and joy, Vi said, "No matter what lies ahead, my darling, each new day brings us closer to God."

Collect all of our Violet products!

A Life of Faith: Violet Travilla Series

MCP
Mission City Press

For more information, write to

Mission City Press at 202 Second Ave. South,
Franklin, Tennessee 37064
or visit our Web Site at:

www.alifeoffaith.com

Collect all of our Elsie products!

A Life of Faith: Elsie Dinsmore Series

* Now Available as a Dramatized Audiobook!

Collect all of our Millie products!

A Life of Faith: Millie Keith Series

✸ Now Available as a Dramatized Audiobook!